Crazy Fox Ranch

D1547185

A Paige MacKenzie Mystery

by

Deborah Garner

Cranberry Cove Press

Crazy Fox Ranch
Deborah Garner

ISBN: 978-0-9969960-4-4

Books by Deborah Garner

The Paige MacKenzie Mystery Series

Above the Bridge
The Moonglow Café
Three Silver Doves
Hutchins Creek Cache
Crazy Fox Ranch

The Moonglow Christmas Novella Series

Mistletoe at Moonglow
Silver Bells at Moonglow
Gingerbread at Moonglow

The Sadie Kramer Flair Series

A Flair for Chardonnay
A Flair for Drama

Cranberry Bluff

For my father,
who always believed in me.

Bruce L. Garner
1922-2017

town site ...
43.73109°N by -110.62847°W

river crossing ...
43.72910°N by -110.66170°W

cattle herd ...
43.64355°N by -110.60497°W

CHAPTER ONE

Paige MacKenzie stood at the top of Teton Pass and looked at the sign before her: *Howdy Stranger, Yonder is Jackson Hole, The Last of the Old West.* If the elevation of 8,431 feet wasn't enough to take her breath away, the view into the valley below was. Even more exhilarating was the adventure ahead. It had taken lots of planning, but she was finally here.

Leaving New York hadn't been easy, even with the lure of the Old West and, even more, the thought of being closer to Jake Norris, her favorite cowboy. Memories from her first trip to Jackson Hole helped as she packed up her Manhattan apartment, changed her reporter status from full time to freelance, and said goodbye to longtime friends and coworkers.

What a fabulous going-away party the office had thrown her, complete with a surprise gift of cowboy boots for her journey. Those boots rested on the passenger seat of her Subaru now, just as they had during the long drive across the country. The car itself was new, too – an all-wheel drive vehicle that would come in handy in the mountains.

Paige pulled her camera from the back seat of the car and took a picture of the welcome sign, as well as several of the views beyond it. All that remained was a short drive down the ten percent grade and she'd be off the road and ready to settle in.

It had been a stroke of good luck that the small cabin she'd stayed in a year before was available. Dan McElroy, the owner, didn't often rent it out. But he'd been delighted when Paige called to say she was coming back to the area. He assured her the cabin would be waiting for her when she arrived. True, Jake had hinted at the idea of her moving into his ranch house, but leaving New York had been a huge enough change. One step at a time, she'd told him.

Taking in a deep breath of clean mountain air, Paige exhaled slowly, got back in her car, and began the steep descent. Sunny skies and clear weather made the drive less difficult than it would have been in rain or snow conditions. Watching her speed carefully on the winding curves, she made it safely to the bottom without incident. She passed through the small town of Wilson, and continued alongside open fields, across the Snake River, and around scenic buttes, until she arrived in Jackson.

The town hadn't changed much since the year before, Paige thought as she drove east along Broadway. The same banks, markets, restaurants and other small businesses flanked the street. Traffic wasn't difficult, thanks to her arrival falling in early May. The busy tourist season had yet to begin, and even that would be easier to navigate than the streets of Manhattan. All in all, she was looking forward to a quieter way of life, and Jackson Hole promised that.

Paige entered the historic section of town and pulled into a parking space across from the town square. Although she was eager to drive north to the cabin, the urge to visit the downtown area for just a few minutes won. She parked the car, stepped out, and looked around. Just as she remembered, shops, cafés, and boutiques surrounded the square. The Million Dollar Cowboy Bar stood out as a central feature.

Paige smiled, thinking back to her last visit. From tidbits of overheard conversation on neighboring bar stools made of horse saddles, to dinner conversation with Jake at the steak house downstairs, "The Cowboy," as locals called it, held plenty of memories.

Crossing the street, Paige entered the town square itself, a square block of scenic park area framed by elk antler arches on each corner. She took a seat on one of the benches that dotted the diagonal walkways and let her thoughts wander.

It would be a big change in lifestyle for her, living in Jackson Hole. The pace was much slower than that in Manhattan. This was something Paige looked forward to. She'd grown fond of the atmosphere of small towns while writing a series of articles about the Old West for *The Manhattan Post*. Aside from being able to spend more time with Jake, she was happy to slow down. She'd put most of her belongings in storage in New York, bringing only the minimum needed for now. To keep her car from being overloaded on the drive, she'd boxed clothing and miscellaneous items and shipped them in advance. Those boxes would be waiting for her at the cabin.

Paige stood again, pondering a desire to linger in town. She looked across to the southeast edge of the square. The Blue Sky Café, her favorite coffee house, would be just around the corner. A vanilla latte sounded tempting, but the urge to get out to the cabin was stronger. She returned to her car and drove north on Cache Street toward Grand Teton National Park.

Just as she remembered from before, her first glimpse of the Tetons amazed her. The mountain range rose from the valley floor with a dramatic presence, a reminder of nature's power and beauty. Again she felt a yearning to pull over and linger, just to take it all in. But she'd have plenty of time for that, now that she'd be staying in the area.

Staying in the area… Paige took another deep breath as she turned right at the Gros Ventre Junction. Was this really home now? That was her intent. The relationship she'd carried on with Jake over the last year had been strong enough to endure the long distance between them. But, as they'd grown closer, the desire to spend more time together had grown stronger and stronger. Realistically, one of them had to make a geographic change. A brief visit to New York from Jake had proven what they both already knew: you could take the cowboy out of the Old West, but you couldn't take the Old West out of the cowboy. Jake had been a fish out of water in Manhattan, just as she'd expected. She still laughed at the image of him trying to hail a cab, as if he were trying to lasso it. It had only made sense for her to move west.

Paige spotted Dan McElroy's property a good half mile before she reached it, his barn standing tall against a clear blue sky. She imagined he'd be working inside, attaching table legs to a carved pine tabletop, putting finishing touches on a log headboard, or sketching new designs for hand-crafted furniture yet to be made. She'd been impressed with his craftsmanship the first time she saw it. Maybe she could manage a purchase or two, small pieces to fit the tiny cabin.

Dan's truck sat in the dirt driveway, not far from the barn. She pulled in next to it, stepped out, and clicked the remote lock on her car out of habit, though she knew there was no reason to do so, not in Jackson Hole, not on Dan's property, at least.

As she expected, she found Dan busy at work inside the barn. The noise of the sander he was using prevented him from hearing her arrive in the doorway, which gave her a chance to lean against the frame and look around. Nothing had changed. A few finished pieces of furniture stood alongside one wall, but the rest of the massive space was filled with works in progress: a rustic coffee table and matching end table, both of pine, a bench of a darker wood of some sort – it was difficult to tell from a distance, and a headboard of elaborate log design. She admired the work, just as she had the first time she'd toured his barn. Dan had an exceptional eye for detail, as well as an artistic sense that suited the mountain area.

The sound of the power tool stopped, and Dan set it aside. He rubbed the nape of his neck and rolled it from side to side, his gaze landing on Paige. "Well, howdy there!" Dan walked to Paige and greeted her with a fatherly hug. "Welcome home, city slicker! It's about time you brought yourself back to Jackson Hole."

Paige laughed. "I can't say I disagree. I've been away too long. Busy with work and travel."

"Yes," Dan said. "Jake keeps me posted on your meanderings: Montana, New Mexico, and Colorado, for your newspaper articles?"

"That sounds right," Paige said. "Plus a few pieces up and down the east coast, whatever the paper needed when I wasn't on the road."

"I guess those'll go by the wayside now? What I understand is you're planning to stay awhile." Dan winked, which caused Paige to blush unexpectedly. She suspected he and Jake shared some guy talk, and couldn't be sure how much detail they got into.

"I won't do the east coast articles, but I'm still going to work freelance on the Old West. There's so much out here for subject matter. I'm looking forward to exploring more of the local history."

This time Dan laughed. "Right, history. From what I hear, you usually find more than that once you start looking around. Mystery and adventure, I believe? Well, there's plenty of that around here. I'm guessing you'll be up to some sort of shenanigans once you get settled in. Speaking of which, let me help you unload your car. The cabin's all ready for you. You even have Internet this time."

"Internet! How wonderful! That'll save me trips into town to use the library's connection. But don't worry about helping unpack the car," Paige said. "I don't have much to bring in."

"Ah, that makes sense," Dan said. "You shipped some boxes out. They're waiting for you in the cabin. I didn't want to leave them on the porch. I'm sure you remember how unpredictable the mountain weather can be."

"I do," Paige said. "The weather forecasts are only good for about twenty-four hours."

"I'd make that about six hours." Dan looked up at the sky. "Today was supposed to be sunny, but I already see clouds forming overhead. My guess is you'll have some rain tonight."

Paige followed Dan's line of sight and had to agree. The puffy white clouds she'd admired earlier were turning gray. "I'd better get moved in, then," she said. "But I can do it myself. Please just keep on with your projects."

"As you wish, my dear." Dan's statement caused Paige to smile. It came across as an odd mix, a formal statement with a mountain man twang to it.

"Still no key?" Paige asked, remembering how surprised she'd been at this before.

'Nope," Dan said. "Just the lock inside. But you let me know if you feel uncomfortable with that. "I can always have a locksmith out to make one."

"I'm sure I'll be fine."

"Well, you let me know if you need anything," Dan said as he turned back toward the work area. "We've got it fixed up a bit for you. You'll see."

CHAPTER TWO

The small cabin beyond Dan's barn appeared just as rustic and charming as Paige remembered it. The front porch served as a wide welcome mat, a rocking chair promising afternoons lost in books, a stack of firewood offering warmth for cool evenings. There was also a wicker chair next to a small table, perfect for company.

Paige approached the cabin with anticipation, excited to start settling in. Parking her car in an open space beside the cabin, she walked around to the front, climbed the few wooden steps to the porch, and stepped through the front door.

At first glance, the interior felt familiar, at least in layout: two rooms – one in front, one just behind it, with a door that she knew led to a bathroom, and a small kitchen area. But the resemblance stopped there. The cabin she'd first entered the previous year had been charming, but bare and had taken some work to fix up. This time, she found upgrades. She suspected she knew exactly what culprits were behind the changes.

Carved lodgepole pine formed a small kitchen table with two stools that could be tucked underneath the table to save space. The chairs near the fireplace in the front room each bore individual details characteristic of hand-crafted furniture. A bookcase to the side of the fireplace offered a selection of reading material. Each piece of furniture featured Dan's handiwork, creative and artistic. The back room held a dresser, exquisite log bed frame and headboard, and matching end tables on each side. She noted the larger bed this time, not the narrow twin that had been there the year before. She smiled. Jake's idea, she suspected.

Paige returned to the front room and observed other details: a vase of wildflowers on the kitchen table, books by her favorite authors in the bookcase – again, Jake's touch – and a western-themed throw rug on the wood plank floor. Her eyes widened with delight at the sight of a small stove in the kitchen area, which Dan had added since her last visit. She'd gotten by with a small electric burner before. But now she'd have the luxury to bake, as well.

"So, what do you think?"

Paige whirled around at the familiar voice, thrilled to see the welcome figure leaning in the doorway. "Jake!" In seconds she was in his arms, wrapped in the soft flannel of his shirt and the security of his embrace. "I've missed you," she whispered, burying her face in his neck.

"Not as much as I've missed you," Jake said. He relaxed his arms, and slid his hands gently up to her shoulders, then her face, and brought her lips to his. Paige felt herself melting. She'd been longing for this exact kiss over the last few weeks.

"So what do you think?" Jake asked, stepping back and extending one arm to indicate the cabin's interior.

"I think you look great," Paige said. And he did. He looked every bit as handsome as the last time she'd seen him – lean and strong, cowboy-handsome in his slim-fitting jeans and boots. A ray of sunlight from the porch backlit his brown hair.

"Not me, the cabin." Jake laughed. "We added a few little improvements."

Paige smiled. "Right. 'A few little improvements,' you say? I'd say you guys turned it into one of those luxury cabins I hear about in this area."

"Maybe just a tad smaller," Jake said. "You're short a few thousand square feet over those upscale dwellings."

"This is plenty of room for me," Paige said, looking around approvingly.

"Just for you?"

"Well maybe for two people, at least sometimes…" Paige smiled, not missing the sly look on Jake's face.

"Like on a cold, rainy night, maybe?" Jake pulled Paige into his arms again.

"I could see that," Paige murmured as Jake placed a soft kiss on her neck. "Or even a warm, sunny afternoon?" She took hold of both his hands and backed slowly toward the other room, smiling.

"I love a girl with mischief on her mind," Jake said as he kicked the cabin door shut and followed.

* * *

"So, how's the construction going at the ranch?"

Paige and Jake sat on the front porch, mugs of freshly brewed coffee in their hands.

"Not bad," Jake said. "Some delays along the way."

"That's normal for construction, isn't it?" Paige asked. "It seems everyone I know who's had some remodeling done has had some sort of setback along the way."

"True." Jake hesitated, took a sip of his coffee. "But it's not just the construction schedule. I can't seem to get that one guy off my back, the one I told you about last week."

"Right," Paige said. "Percy something or other?"

Jake nodded. "Percy Carter."

"The one who wants to buy your property, even though it's not for sale?"

"That's the one."

"But you told him you weren't looking to sell it. And he's still bothering you?" Paige sighed. "Some people just can't take 'no' for an answer."

"I guess not," Jake said. "I've told him at least three times that the ranch is not for sale. Last time he asked, I emphasized that there was no point in coming back to discuss it again."

"You think he'll give up?" Paige tilted her head to the side, her auburn hair cascading over her shoulder. "He sounds persistent."

"I'd say downright pig-headed is more like it," Jake said. "And, unfortunately, I doubt he'll give up. I don't understand it. There are other properties around that *are* for sale. Why chase after this one?"

"Good question," Paige said. "Did you ask him?"

"Of course I did. He says he just likes this particular location."

Paige shrugged. "Well, he should have grabbed it when it was for sale before you bought it. If I recall, it had been on the market for a long time."

"Exactly," Jake said. "He had his chance before. I told him so, too, even asked why he didn't buy it back then. I couldn't get a decent answer out of him."

"That's strange." Paige leaned forward, elbows on her knees, hands wrapped around the coffee mug. "You'd think he could say why he passed it up before, or at least explain the sudden interest."

"Makes no sense to me," Jake said. "But he's a strange guy. Comes on real friendly, and then turns harsh quickly. Every time he stops by, it's the same routine." Jake finished his coffee, and set the mug down on the little table. He stood up and stretched both arms over his head. Paige caught her breath. Every time she saw him, his lean, lanky body was more appealing.

"Couldn't help hearing that last comment." Paige and Jake looked up to see Dan approaching. "You must be talking about Percy Carter."

"Good guess," Jake said. He shook Dan's hand. "That's exactly who we're talking about. I was just telling Paige that he's still after me to sell him my property."

"That's not your plan, I take it," Dan said. "All that construction would be a waste if you up and sold the ranch. Every time I drive by, some machine or other is digging up a new area."

"Of course Jake's not selling it," Paige said, looking up at the two men. "He's turning it into..." She paused and looked at Jake, unsure how much of his plans he'd disclosed to others.

"A guest ranch," Dan said. "I know that. Jake and I've had discussions about it over a few beers at the Cowboy. That's why I'd be shocked if he agreed to sell."

"Oh, the Million Dollar Cowboy Bar!" Paige said. She looked at Jake and smiled. "I think I'll need to see that place again. I remember sitting on one of those horse saddles at the bar last year."

"And eavesdropping on other customers, if I recall," Jake said. He turned to Dan. "It's one of her special skills. Gets her in trouble sometimes, too."

"Well, life's no fun without a little trouble now and then," Dan said. "Speaking of trouble *and* Percy Carter, I don't trust that guy to leave you alone. I'd be careful."

"Any particular reason?" Paige asked. She stood up to feel less like both men were towering over her. It didn't help much.

Dan shook his head. "Just gut instinct. Nothing I can put my finger on. He hangs out in town. Most of the local bartenders know him. Never causes a scene, but he watches people. Closely. Like he's looking for someone or something."

"No crime in hanging out in town or in watching people," Jake said.

"You're right," Dan said. "But something about him seems sketchy. I'd be cautious, especially if he's coming onto your property."

"I've asked him not to come back," Jake said. "Hopefully that'll be the end of it."

Paige looked at Dan. "I don't understand why he didn't buy the ranch before Jake got to it. Do you have any idea why he didn't snatch it up, Dan?"

"Well, Percy Carter only showed up recently, not long after Jake bought the ranch. I don't think he knew anyone had bought it. He may not even have known it was for sale. Not sure why else he's here. He's not a local. Doesn't have family here, either, that I know of."

"Where's he from?" Paige looked from Jake to Dan.

"Not sure," Dan said.

"Somewhere out west," Jake said. "That's all he says."

"I thought *this* was 'out west,'" Paige said.

"Well, this is the *real* West." Dan laughed. "The *Old* West. But we don't exactly have oceanfront property here, so I'm thinking he's from west of the Old West."

Paige nodded, thinking. "So he could be from any number of places west of here. Idaho? Oregon? California, maybe? Or he could be lying altogether."

"Wouldn't surprise me," Jake said. "I don't get a single good feeling about the guy. No reason I should expect him to be honest. Nothing he says sounds up front to me. Like how he won't tell me why he wants my ranch so much."

"Weird that he wouldn't give you a reason," Paige said.

"Yep. Just kept repeating that it was the perfect spot," Jake said.

"Which it is," Paige mused.

"Sure," Dan said. "But there are plenty of 'perfect spots' in this valley. Hard to find one that isn't. Makes no sense to go after a property that isn't for sale."

"So, he has an ulterior motive," Paige said, talking more to herself than anyone else. "Wonder what it could be…"

"Paige," Jake said quickly, "please don't start." He looked at Dan. "She has the sleuthing gene, you know. Hasn't even been here twenty-four hours, and she's found herself a mystery to solve."

"Ah, yes," Dan said. "You've told me some stories about that."

"OK, both of you," Paige said, ignoring the references to previous adventures spurred on by her inquisitive nature. "You can't tell me you aren't curious why this guy keeps hanging around, can you?"

Dan shrugged his shoulders. "I'm not curious. I think the guy should leave Jake alone, that's all. Anyway, I've got to get back to work on a lodgepole pine chair I promised a lady up in Pilgrim Creek. Just wanted to make sure you were settling in OK, Paige." He lifted one hand in a wave of departure as he turned away.

"I'm not sure I'm curious, either, or that I even care," Jake said. "I just want him to stop pestering me about selling the property. Hopefully he will now. I made myself pretty clear." He pulled the keys to his truck out of his pocket. "I've got to get back to the ranch to meet the contractor. How about coming over in a bit, so I can show you the progress on the ranch?" He leaned forward and gave her a tender kiss.

"Absolutely." Paige smiled. "Give me an hour to unpack a few things."

"Deal," Jake said.

Paige watched him climb in his truck and back out of the driveway. She took both empty coffee mugs and headed inside the cabin. Paige sighed as she set the mugs in the small sink, her instincts sending up a red flag. *I have a feeling this Percy Carter situation isn't over.*

CHAPTER THREE

Paige turned right out of Dan McElroy's driveway and headed east toward the small town of Kelly, a hamlet that consisted of not much more than a post office, a coffee and sandwich café, and a handful of cabins and yurts. Kelly had been a growing community earlier in Jackson Hole's history until a flood in 1927 essentially wiped the town out, at the same time creating Slide Lake, farther east, as well as a fascinating geological rock area formed by the earthquake-induced flood. She reminded herself to get out to the trail that meandered through that site.

She stopped at the Kelly post office and dropped a postcard in the mail drop. She'd promised Susan, the editor for *The Manhattan Post*, that she'd send her the occasional postcard for her collection. She'd also write her an email later to let her know she'd arrived safely. She would be sure to keep in touch. Not only was Susan a good friend after all these years of working together, but Paige hoped Susan would start assigning her freelance work sooner than later.

Continuing on, she spotted Jake's ranch from a distance. The western archway above the driveway that was her original landmark on her first visit was missing, but the assortment of work vehicles parked in front of and on the property made her certain she had the right place. The CAT equipment surprised her somehow. She couldn't help but laugh at herself, knowing the mental image she'd had of the construction work hadn't gone much beyond hammers and nails. How silly of her. Of course, her experience of "construction" went no further than attempting to replace a broken towel bar in her bathroom. Jake had spared her most of the work details, other than saying he'd found an excellent contractor, and he knew Paige would be excited to see the progress when she arrived. But it was a large property, with five cabins being updated to accommodate overnight guests. In addition, the main ranch house itself was being remodeled so that the lower half could be used as a lodge, while the upper level could serve as Jake's private residence. It was only natural that large equipment would be needed for some of the tasks. Converting the property into a guest ranch was a huge endeavor.

Paige signaled left, turned into the dusty driveway, and followed its sage-brush-flanked path up to the ranch house. She parked her car and stepped outside, looking around. A half dozen construction crew workers toiled on projects around the property. Two worked on the roof of a far cabin. Several were lowering long pipes into a ditch alongside the closest cabin. One more worked on the fence around the property, and yet another operated one of the heavier pieces of machinery not far from the main ranch house. The noise from that particular machine explained why Jake wasn't in the open doorway. There was no way he could have heard her car approaching over the commotion.

Climbing the steps to the massive porch, Paige entered the house, expecting to see Jake in some sort of meeting with his contractor. What was the guy's name? Chris something-or-other, she recalled from a few statements relayed across the miles while she was still in New York. "Chris came highly recommended." "Chris has a good idea about revamping the living room." That sort of thing. She'd been pleased that Jake had found someone with a good, dependable reputation. She'd heard enough horror stories about construction problems – over budget, poor workmanship, wrong supplies ordered. There were so many ways a big project could go wrong.

She'd envisioned a rough, weathered man, someone tan and strong, probably older, since he had lots of experience with western construction and design. Hence it was a surprise – make that a shock – to find Jake hunched over his dining room table, shoulder to shoulder with a woman in tight blue jeans, a slim-fitting white T-shirt, and a voluminous length of blonde hair snaking down her back. Only work boots and a hard hat in her right hand hinted that she belonged in the scene. Had Paige not been certain she'd turned into the correct driveway, she might have thought she'd entered the wrong property.

Hearing footsteps, Jake turned, his face lighting up at the sight of Paige. "There you are! Come on in. Chris and I were just discussing an adjustment to one of the cabins."

Chris? This was Chris, the contractor? "Oh," Paige said. "You're Jake's contractor?" She tried for nonchalant. "I thought all contractors were beefy men with gray beards."

"Not me. But I've got a head for plans and am mad for deadlines," Chris said. Her smile was pageant worthy, her skin flawless, her eyes a stunning blue and – *seriously?* – she had dimples that made her somehow more attractive than she already was. Paige resisted the impulse to glance at Chris's figure, knowing it would be downright rude. Paige squirmed a little at the mild streak of unexpected jealousy shooting through her. It wasn't necessary to look. Paige knew she faced physical perfection.

"Paige MacKenzie," she said.

Chris placed a slender but calloused hand in Paige's and gave a firm shake. "Christine Farrell."

"Chris*tine*..." Paige repeated, maintaining her smile.

"Yes, Paige," Jake said, noting Paige's odd behavior. "This is Chris, the contractor I told you about." His eyebrows lifted, as if questioning Paige's memory.

"Of course!" Paige said. "*Chris*, your *contractor*." She tried not to flinch at her excessive response. It was almost involuntary. She turned to Chris. "It's nice to meet you. Are you a Jackson Hole native?"

"No. I'm from Idaho Falls. But I'm living on the property for the duration of this project, thank heavens. I'd have a 200 mile round trip commute, otherwise," Chris said. "Jake's told me all about you." Silver cowboy boot earrings reflected sunlight from a front window as they dangled from her earlobes.

"Mostly good, I hope." Paige kept her tone light.

"Of course!" Chris gushed. "He's been so excited about your arrival." She glanced at Jake with what Paige interpreted to be an adoring smile, though she was aware she might be projecting.

"Come see what we're working on," Jake said. He motioned Paige over, gave her a kiss and indicated blueprints on the table.

Several large sheets of paper sat in a stacked pile. The first showed a layout of the entire ranch, the perimeter of the property marked, the individual buildings detailed with measurements. Lower sheets showed closer views of different buildings, the first being the main ranch house, several others indicating cabins already existing. Although Paige had limited experience reading blueprints, she could spot proposed extensions on some of the structures.

"It looks like you're expanding a couple of the buildings," Paige said.

"Yes," Jake said. "The cabins now are single rooms, but I want some to be able to accommodate families – a bedroom for the parents, a second room for kids, and a main room large enough to hold a fold-out couch."

"Smart," Paige said, nodding as she looked over the blueprints. "With all these options, you'll have a wider range of guests. You'll have a couple of small cabins for cozy romantic getaways, while providing others large enough for families or groups of friends."

"Exactly," Jake said.

"Jake wants the ranch to be family friendly," Chris said enthusiastically. "So we've designed some of the cabins for that purpose."

"I see," Paige said. She wondered exactly how this statement differed from what Jake had just said. Yet Chris appeared pleased to have contributed to the conversation, or at least to think she had.

A worker in dusty overalls stuck his head inside the front door. "Chris, one of the guys working on Cabin 4 has an electrical question."

"Be right there," Chris said as the man ducked back outside. "It's always something." She picked up a small notepad and pen from the table and stuffed them into an already tight T-shirt pocket. "It was great meeting you, Paige." She turned toward Jake and flashed a smile. "I'll be outside if you need me for anything."

"So," Paige said, eager to turn the conversation away from the flirtatious contractor, "show me what you've done inside here. The house has a delicious aroma of sawdust."

"Yes," Jake beamed. "It's just another bonus we'll be offering."

"Be serious," Paige said.

Jake pulled Paige into his arms and kissed her tenderly. "How's that for serious?" he whispered, his lips brushing against her ear.

"Better," Paige murmured. "But I still want to see the progress you've made in here."

"Right this way."

Following Jake, Paige took a tour of the house, starting first with the kitchen, where the stove and refrigerator had been replaced by larger, industrial models. The sawdust she'd picked up on from the front room dotted the floor, remnants of counters that had been cut back to make room for the new equipment.

"Getting ready to do some cooking?"

"Breakfast," Jake explained. "Guests on a ranch deserve a good old-fashioned western breakfast. Hearty stuff to prepare them for a day in the wilderness."

"The wilderness?" Paige laughed, though she immediately recognized her reaction as ridiculous. In spite of the commercial aspects of the town and tourist activities, there was plenty of wilderness in Jackson Hole. It only took a short drive or hike to be completely surrounded by nature. "So you're planning to serve breakfast. Any other meals?"

"We'll see," Jake said. "Right now breakfast is the plan. There are plenty of restaurants in the area for lunch and dinners, and places to pick up picnic supplies if guests plan to spend time up in the parks."

"True," Paige agreed. "I think breakfast is a great idea. The overnight guests are here already. Why not feed them and give them a good start to their day? I take it you'll hire a cook?"

"What? You aren't going to fix breakfast for everyone?" Jake tried to look serious but failed.

"If toast, yogurt and orange juice will fill the bill, I could probably manage." Paige laughed. Although she liked to bake, she was the first to admit that the idea of cooking for more than two or three people did not appeal to her.

"I'm thinking more along the lines of pancakes, omelets, bacon, sausage and ham, personally," Jake said. "And I'll be interviewing for a cook, so you're off the hook."

"Well, that's a relief," Paige said. "I suppose you'll be hiring quite a few people. It'll take some work to keep up with the place, especially after you open."

Jake picked up a nail off the floor and set it on a counter. "Yes, not only the cook, but a housekeeper to clean the cabins between guests, a wrangler for the horses, and a maintenance/security person. Of course, I could also use a personal assistant to help me keep track of the business side of things, plus miscellaneous details around the place. Someone I can work with closely."

"Just how closely?" Paige said.

Jake wrapped his arm around Paige's waist and drew her against him. He brushed his lips against her cheek before whispering in her ear. "This closely…"

"Well, in that case, maybe I should apply for the job."

"Maybe you should."

"What does it pay?" Paige fought to maintain the serious tone one might use in a job interview, but it wasn't easy with Jake now kissing her neck.

"I haven't finished the budget yet," Jake whispered, "but I expect there would be all sorts of fringe benefits."

"Free breakfast?" Paige ran a variety of perks through her mind that she might request.

"I think that could be arranged," Jake said. He slipped her T-shirt over one shoulder and brushed his lips against her skin.

"Only if you add waffles to the breakfast menu," Paige said. "With berries and whipped cream. And real maple syrup."

"Now you're getting demanding." Jake laughed as he readjusted the neckline of Paige's T-shirt and kissed her forehead.

"I know," Paige said. "See what a nuisance I could be to have around?"

"A lovely nuisance," Jake replied.

"Hey, Jake?" Chris was back in the house. "We need to get the electrician back out here for Cabin 4."

"Set it up," Jake said matter-of-factly.

"All right. Thought I'd let you know that AJ's schedule is a little different than the other guys'. Some days, he may be working late, even past dusk, so don't worry if you see his lights or hear his banging on the fence."

Paige stepped back into the front room as Jake and Chris discussed the details of the cabin's electrical needs and other project plans, Chris standing closer than necessary. *I have no reason to be jealous,* Paige scolded herself. It wasn't like her to feel insecure about anything. If anything, she'd been the one to insist on keeping her independence, despite Jake's attempts to persuade her otherwise. But the move to Jackson Hole from New York wasn't a small step. And now she was here, with him. And with a contractor who could have just stepped off a runway for Victoria's Secret. *Tsk, tsk.* She chastised herself again. *Stop being ridiculous.* Maybe she was just tired from the long days on the road. She'd feel better once she got a full night's sleep.

"It's always something," Jake said as he reentered the front room. "If not electrical, then plumbing or a mistake in a materials delivery. Not to mention inspections and delays." He sounded resigned, yet not discouraged. "It's fine, it's just how it goes."

"Well, you have time," Paige said. "You're not opening until next summer, right?"

Jake nodded. "Technically, you're right. We won't take bookings until then. But we're having that open house next week."

Paige had contemplated the idea when he first told her about it. It was a good one. It would allow Jake to incorporate any comments or suggestions that came up before the official opening.

"I think that's great." Paige ran possibilities through her mind, both for the open house and for the full opening the following summer. There were many ways to create publicity for the ranch. She made a mental note to contact the local paper, as well as travel websites. Maybe marketing the ranch was one of the ways she truly could assist Jake.

"It's also practical," Jake added. "We need to get through all the construction this summer. Winters here are too difficult. So planning the open house gave us a deadline to get a few of the cabins ready."

"And it will help avoid last minute problems next spring, when you'll already have reservations booked," Paige said. "I hope this works out."

"I'm sure it will," Jake said, looking up as Chris entered the room, clipboard in hand. "I have a competent contractor who'll make sure we pull this off."

"Absolutely." Chris beamed as she directed a radiant smile toward Paige.

"And I now have an extremely competent personal assistant, as well," Jake added, wrapping his arm around Paige and pulling her close.

"I believe you do," Paige said. She was certain she saw Chris's perfect smile momentarily waiver.

CHAPTER FOUR

Paige looked up and down the bar counter, amazed. "You say there are 2,032 of these silver dollars here?"

"Yep," Jake said as he handed the bartender a twenty. "All uncirculated 1921 Morgans, too. From the Denver Mint. Ever heard of that place?" He grinned as Paige teasingly smacked his arm. He was well aware she'd visited the Mint recently on an assignment in Colorado. He'd been with her.

"Very funny," Paige said. She sipped her white wine and glanced around. "So this is the Silver Dollar Bar. Very cool place."

"That it is." Jake took a swig of his Snake River Lager draft and set the glass down on the counter. "It's been here since ...the fifties?" He directed his question to the bartender, a fellow wearing a vest and a nametag that said "Spec."

The bartender nodded. "Yep, 1950. The bar is part of The Wort Hotel. Charles Wort purchased four lots for twenty-five dollars each. His sons, John and Jess, built the hotel in 1941 after he passed away. You should check out the framed articles in the hallway. Lots of interesting information."

"Any ghosts?" Paige asked.

"Ghosts?" Jake repeated, giving Paige a look.

"Yes, Jake, ghosts," Paige said. "It's not that odd a question. Some historic hotels do have a history of ghosts." She ignored Jake and waited for the bartender to answer.

"Who knows?" Spec shrugged, but Paige was certain he winked. He turned and walked away as another customer waved an empty glass in the air.

"In any case, it's a great historic hotel and bar," Jake continued. "Pretty much the town meeting place. People simply say, 'Meet me at the Wort,' and everyone knows where to go. You'll see a lot of locals here. Some of them are real characters."

"I noticed that when I walked down the hallway," Paige said. "One guy in particular struck me as a character. He was just standing in front of a photograph, but he stared at it intently."

"Like people do in an art museum, or a gallery?" Jake accepted change from the bartender and set a tip on the counter before pocketing the rest.

"No, not exactly." Paige thought over her impression of the man she'd seen, trying to pinpoint what seemed odd to her. "He was analyzing it, looking for some detail in it. It was almost as if he wanted to climb into the picture so that he could search the ground or the people for something."

"Strange," Jake said, "but not that big a deal, I don't think. Those photographs catch people's attention all the time. Which one was it?"

"I didn't take a close look at the picture, just the guy looking at it, since his behavior seemed weird." Paige said. "The photo was of a man on a horse, I think."

"Alan Ladd?" Jake took another swig of beer.

"The movie star from the fifties?" Paige raised her eyebrows. "I don't know. I passed by quickly so the guy didn't think I wanted to start a conversation." She paused. "Yes, come to think of it, it was Alan Ladd."

"Ah," Jake said. "That picture is from the movie, *Shane*. It was filmed in Jackson Hole. Visitors ask about it all the time."

"Right," Paige said. "I remember reading about that when I first researched the area. A lot of movies have been filmed here. Isn't that right?"

"Absolutely," Jake said. "Not only *Shane*, but many others. *The Big Trail*, with John Wayne, for example. That was his first leading role."

"Really?" Paige's eyebrows rose in surprise.

"*Spencer's Mountain* was filmed here, too, with Henry Fonda and Maureen O'Hara," Jake continued. "And *Any Which Way You Can*, with Clint Eastwood. Others, too."

"Well, well," Paige said, smiling. "I didn't know you were such a film buff."

"Heck, yeah," Jake said. "When it comes to those old westerns I am."

"Not sure I've seen all those." Paige took a sip of wine and set the glass down on one of the embedded silver dollars in the bar top.

"Sounds like a movie marathon night is in order," Jake said. "A cozy one, maybe?" A sly smile crossed his face.

"You do want me to watch the movies, don't you?" Paige smiled. Jake suddenly reminded her of a high school kid asking a crush to the local theater, with anything but watching the movie on his mind.

"Actually, yes, you should watch them," Jake said. "These are classics. Everyone should see them at least once.

I've probably seen *Shane* twenty times." He picked up his beer glass. "I especially love the part where…" He paused as Paige tugged on his shirt sleeve.

"That's the guy I was talking about," Paige said, nodding toward the door to the bar. A man had just stepped inside.

Jake set the glass back down abruptly with a sharp clink that turned a few heads on nearby bar stools. "That's the guy," he said.

"Right," Paige said. "The one who was staring at that photograph."

"No," Jake said. "I mean that's the guy who's been after me to sell him the ranch."

"Really?" Paige watched while the man scouted around for a seat. He looked to be in his seventies, a bit scruffy. He didn't quite fit in as a local. He seemed to lock eyes with Jake, but turned away and chose to sit at a far table. Paige breathed a sigh of relief, glad to avoid a potential public confrontation. "Well, Dan did say the guy hangs out a lot at Jackson Hole bars."

"When he's not hovering around my place, that is." Jake's tone was less than amused.

"Well, hopefully he got the message when you told him not to come back," Paige said. "It seems pointless to pursue buying a property that isn't for sale, especially when the owner has firmly told you to stay away."

"I'd say 'firmly' is an understatement," Jake said.

Paige frowned. "You didn't threaten him, did you? He sounds like the unpredictable sort."

"Of course not," Jake said. "I did tell him I would contact the authorities if he came on my property again, but I don't see that as a threat."

"Hopefully he doesn't either," Paige said. "It seems perfectly reasonable to ask someone not to trespass. Maybe you should put up a 'No Trespassing' sign. Wait." Paige corrected herself quickly. "That's not smart, at least not in the long run. That would hardly be a welcome sign to guests. But you could put it up while you're finishing construction."

"Not a bad idea," Jake said as he looked around the bar. "Looks like Carter left."

Paige glanced over her shoulder, and noticed Carter's table was now empty. "Huh," she said. "Didn't even stay long enough for a drink. Or…" She paused as a server passed by with a huge plate of nachos. "…or something to eat." After the tempting food was out of sight and scent, she turned back to Jake. "I hope he's not following you, like a stalker."

"I don't think so, Paige," Jake said. "He's only approached me at home. Don't start imagining things. You haven't even unpacked and you're already looking for some sort of puzzle to solve."

"I have so unpacked," Paige insisted just before remembering several boxes still in the trunk of her car. "Mostly." She tilted her head to the side and ran a finger down Jake's arm. "Besides, I've been too distracted to get into mischief yet."

Jake finished off his beer, and set the glass down with a hearty laugh. "The operative word being 'yet.' Paige, I swear 'trouble' is your middle name. You're never too distracted to find trouble. And if you're not looking for it, it finds you."

"OK, you have a point." Paige sighed. She could hardly deny it. He'd watched her get tangled up in precarious situations several times. She stood up and pushed her empty wine glass toward the far side of the bar, where it would be easy for the bartender to retrieve. "I'm going to take a closer look at that photograph. Care to join me?"

Without waiting for Jake's reply, Paige left for the hallway with the framed photographs. Sure enough, the photo in question was Alan Ladd, saddled up and looking down at smiling co-star Jean Arthur. The Teton mountain range formed a spectacular background for the wilderness scene.

"And this photo is also from *Shane*," Paige said, moving on to another. A small placard by each photo identified which movie it was from.

"Yep," Jake said. "That's the famous fight scene. Lots of great scenes and lines in that film."

"And this one?" Paige leaned in to read the note by another framed picture.

"*Spencer's Mountain*," Jake said. "Excellent film with Henry Fonda. The TV show *The Waltons* was based on the same book as the movie. And there's a shot from *The Big Trail* over here." They moved from one photo to the next.

"OK," Paige said. "You're on for a movie marathon. I'll bring the popcorn."

CHAPTER FIVE

A light evening breeze flowed across the porch as Paige stepped outside the door of her cabin and sat in the rocking chair. Forgoing her usual habit of carrying a book with her, or a writing notebook, she simply rocked and enjoyed the wind brushing across her face. She closed her eyes and let her mind wander, tendrils of hair caressing her neck.

The twilight hour was cool, but not chilly; quiet, but not silent. She let her back sink against the strong backing of the wooden chair. Although she was alone, Dan's solid craftsmanship gave her a sense of security and peace. She acknowledged one of those rare perfect moments, when all stress fades away and only calm exists.

Against Jake's not-too-subtle, yet gracious protests, she'd chosen to spend her first night alone in the cabin. Delighted as she was to see Jake, the long drive, the visit to Jake's ranch, and the outing to the Silver Dollar Bar had drained the last of her energy. She looked forward to starting in on her newly acquired position of ranch assistant – unofficial though it may be – but not before a good night's sleep. Besides, her thoughts were already in a flurry with just the first day's observations.

During phone calls, emails, and texts, Jake had mentioned various aspects of the work but had saved details, telling her she'd see firsthand when she arrived. Their conversations and correspondence leaned more toward the personal, about missing each other, about how soon they'd be together, about how her arrangements for the move were coming along.

Now that she'd seen the ranch, she had to admit she was impressed. Jake's casual comments about having the floors refinished and fixing a crooked beam here or there were modest in comparison to how much work had been done. The upgrading of the property was substantial. Even with lingering sawdust and ongoing projects, it was obvious a lot had been accomplished. *I suppose this is one advantage of having a great contractor.*

Paige opened her eyes as she thought about her first encounter with Chris...or Christine. She sat up straighter. To say she'd been surprised would be an understatement though she tried hard to avoid stereotypes. There was no reason a woman who could feasibly snag a Miss America title couldn't be a top-notch construction contractor. And clearly she was. The guest ranch was coming along right on schedule. And Jake had said it was even under budget.

Paige leaned back again and relaxed. She didn't really feel jealous, just caught off guard. Even across the miles, spending months apart between trips out West, she'd never worried about Jake's fidelity. He'd made his feelings clear. She knew he wanted a committed relationship, and had waited patiently while Paige wrestled with the decision to move to Jackson Hole.

Her train of thought switched to a replay of the visit to the Silver Dollar Bar and the movie photographs they'd seen in the hallway. The history of Hollywood involvement in Jackson Hole intrigued her. It was a great angle for an article to pitch to Susan. But seeing the man there who'd been bothering Jake intrigued her even more. Jake had said his name was Percy Carter. Maybe she could find out more about him. It was something Jake wouldn't think to do – he just wanted the guy to stay away – but it was second nature to her as a reporter.

Moving inside, Paige set up her laptop at the small kitchen table, grateful for the Internet access that Dan had arranged. She hadn't minded working at the library on her first trip to Jackson, but the quick access to research and email without having to drive into town was a definite plus.

While her laptop warmed up, she built a small fire in the fireplace. The evening promised to be cool enough to merit some warmth, and the comforting ambiance of a fire was appealing.

With the fire beginning to catch, she moved to the kitchen area and looked over her dinner options. Her choices appeared to be soup, soup, or soup, based on canned items she'd brought with her on her road trip. She'd go shopping the next day.

As lentil soup warmed on the stove, she sat at the kitchen table and checked her email. Susan had sent a one-line response to Paige's earlier message, saying she was glad Paige had made it safely across the country.

Paige returned to the stove, and pulled the lightly bubbling saucepan of soup off the heated burner and onto a cool one. She chose a blue glazed pottery bowl, rinsed it out, poured the hot soup into it, and then she set the bowl on the table, angling her laptop off to the side. A cold bottle of water from the refrigerator completed the meal.

Settling in at the table, she glanced at the fireplace, pleased to see her quick combination of nearby ingredients had served its purpose. It was just another of Dan's many thoughtful preparations, having newspaper, kindling and firewood on hand. She took a spoonful of soup, blew across it to cool it, and enjoyed a first taste as she hit 'reply' to prepare an answer to Susan's email.

Susan,

I'm enjoying a first evening alone in Dan McElroy's cabin. He — and Jake, I'm sure — have outfitted the place with everything I need from furniture, to firewood, to miscellaneous items like soup bowls and linens. Tomorrow when I go to town, I'll stock up on other supplies, especially groceries. As you know, I shipped some boxes out here in advance, plus tucked some in the car. Those are all waiting to be unloaded, a task I'll also try to tackle tomorrow.

I know you said to take time to settle in before I thought about feature topics, but I happened to stumble into something today that I think would interest readers. There's a fascinating history of Hollywood filming in Jackson Hole. It goes back as far as silent films, and continues up to current times. Many are well-known classic westerns, such as Shane *and* Spencer's Mountain. *But there are smaller films, too, as well as a variety of television episodes. What do you think? I'm curious about this myself, so I'll look into it in case it's something you'd like for* The Post.

I'll have more to say once I get settled. I do miss everyone there. Please say hi for me!

Paige

With a quick click, Paige sent the email to Susan and closed the laptop. She finished the soup, moved the bowl and spoon to the sink, and was about to change into a nightshirt when a knock at the front door startled her. *Jake*, she thought, laughing inwardly at the thought he couldn't bear to leave her alone for the night. She opened the door with a huge grin that faltered only slightly at the sight of Dan holding out a small paper bag.

"From Judy," Dan explained, as if that would make sense.

Paige tumbled the name around in her memory, not connecting it with anyone. "Do I know Judy?"

"Judy, from the Blue Sky Café," Dan said. "Oh, wait. You haven't met her yet. She's the new owner."

"Oh, OK," Paige said. Of course there was someone new running the place. She knew, Maddie, the previous owner of her favorite Jackson Hole café, had moved on. "Well, thank you, that's very thoughtful of her, though I have a feeling you're the one I should thank, for bringing it to me." Paige looked inside the bag and leaned forward to breathe in the aroma. "Yum, freshly baked blueberry muffins. I'll have one with coffee in the morning."

A pleased smile spread across Dan's face. "Exactly what I told her, that you'd want something sweet to start off your first full day here."

"Well," Paige said. "I'm glad she listened to you."

Dan's expression grew curiously impish. "Oh, she pretty much always listens to me." He lowered his voice and leaned forward, even though there was no one anywhere near. "I think she's sweet on me, you see."

"Aha," Paige said, noting a faint blush on Dan's face. "And you on her, I suspect."

Dan coughed and stood up straight. "Well, I'm not sure about that. But she's a mighty nice lady. Makes a mean peach pie, too."

"I see," Paige said, trying not to laugh. "Well that's always a plus, a good peach pie."

"You bet it is," Dan said. "And don't you go teasing me now." Although he was trying to be serious, there was a twinkle in Dan's eye.

"I wouldn't think of it," Paige said. "And I truly appreciate the blueberry muffins. Very thoughtful of you. Of both of you."

"You're welcome," Dan said. He tipped an imaginary hat and walked back toward the main farmhouse.

Paige closed the door and put the bag with the muffins on the counter, beside the coffeemaker. She was glad to see the hint of a romantic relationship in Dan's life. He was a good man, caring and giving, in addition to being creative and hardworking. He deserved to be happy, and although he'd never struck her as unhappy, this new enthusiasm was welcome.

She set up the coffeemaker for the morning, so she'd only have to click the switch to start it when she woke up. Then Paige retired to the back room and sorted through a stack of yet unpacked clothing. She pulled on a pale blue cotton nightshirt, worn soft with age. Climbing into bed, she picked up a book from the bedside table, ready for her nightly habit of reading in bed. A half page in, her eyelids drifted downward and she was fast asleep.

CHAPTER SIX

Paige sat up, stretched, and noticed it was barely past six o'clock. She wasn't surprised. Yesterday had worn her out, so she'd fallen asleep early, easily getting nine hours of sleep.

When she pulled aside the curtains in the back room, instead of bright rays of sunshine, she saw light softened by gray clouds and a faint fog. Ah, mountain weather, she reminded herself, always unpredictable.

In the front room, she switched on the coffeemaker and felt grateful at this simple convenience. As the cabin filled with the scent of French roast, she turned on her laptop and set one of the muffins on a plate.

Minutes later, coffee in hand, she checked email and found a reply from Susan, who had probably already been working for an hour or so since she was an early riser and in a time zone two hours ahead.

Paige,

I'm so glad the drive went well and that you're safely in Jackson Hole. I'll bet Jake is thrilled to have you close. We all miss you already, of course, but I plan to keep you busy still working for The Post, *which is one way I'll be able to keep up with you and your adventures.*

A feature on the filming history in that part of Wyoming sounds intriguing. But take your time. Rest. I trust you to find the most interesting tidbits for our readers. Take care.

Susan

Paige smiled as she savored her coffee and took a bite of blueberry muffin. She'd barely arrived in Jackson Hole and already had an assignment – multiple assignments, really: assisting Jake with the ranch, researching an article for Susan, and…well, it wasn't really an assignment, but she wasn't about to ignore the Percy Carter situation. Something wasn't right about the way he'd been pressuring Jake to sell his property, especially now that Paige had seen him in person. Her instincts were almost always on target, and this time they told her something shady was up. Aside from her own curiosity, she didn't like the thought of someone interfering with Jake's efforts to get the guest ranch up and running.

Closing down her laptop, Paige finished her coffee and muffin, and washed the plate and mug. She returned to the back room and sifted through her clothes, unfolding and hanging up a few pieces that she hadn't yet removed from her suitcase. A glance out the window reminded her of the overcast weather, so she chose to wear layers: a deep green T-shirt that matched her eyes, favorite jeans, and a navy blue zippered New York Yankees hoodie, just in case she faced an impromptu mountain downpour. Adding her most comfortable walking shoes, she grabbed her purse and left the cabin.

She nearly turned right at the end of the driveway toward Jake's ranch. She knew he'd be happy if she dropped in to see him after he'd respected her wishes to have a night alone at the cabin. But the draw toward the town of Jackson won out. She wanted to stop by the Blue Sky Café, and she was itching to start researching the filming history in the area. She drove into town, found a parking spot near the town square and walked the short distance to the café.

Paige smiled as she approached the café, the familiar sight of the log cabin bringing back memories of easy mornings reading the local paper. The rustic appeal of the old doorway was inviting. Wind chimes hung from a tree branch in a small front garden, brushing softly against each other. Customers sat at tables inside the front windows. A "Help Wanted" sign hung in one glass pane. Pottery filled with brightly colored annuals flanked three steps leading up to the door.

Paige assumed the woman standing behind the counter was Judy, the new owner. She was about Dan's age, and she was instructing two younger baristas who were preparing drinks for customers. The café's décor hadn't changed since Paige's last visit. It still had the sense of a cabin interior. The small table and chair she'd occupied on her first visit remained in the same place, as did a booth in the far back corner, where she'd first spotted Jake about a year ago.

She joined the line and surveyed the offerings behind a glass partition, wishing suddenly that she'd saved the blueberry muffin she'd consumed for later. The selection was decadent: cinnamon rolls covered with icing, raspberry scones – admittedly her latest favorite – orange-lemon tea cakes, and a variety of croissants with assorted fillings. She was reading the ingredients on a vegan apple turnover when she reached the front of the line.

"Good morning," the woman said. Her nametag verified that this was Judy. "You must be Paige MacKenzie. Dan told me you were arriving yesterday."

"Yes, I am," Paige said. "How did you know?"

Judy, a short, trim woman, pointed just to below Paige's shoulder in explanation.

Paige looked down at her sweatshirt. She'd forgotten about the logo. She laughed. "Ah, yes, New York Yankees. One of several goodbye gifts from coworkers."

"And the fancy camera," Judy added. "These days, most tourists just use their phones."

"Right." Paige nodded. "Reporter's habit. I'd hate to miss a photo op around here. You never know if a moose might come into view. Or a stately buck, for that matter."

"Exactly," Judy said. "In fact, there could be one right behind you and you wouldn't even know it." Her eyes shifted mischievously to the side. Paige turned to follow the direction of Judy's glance.

"Jake! I didn't see you come in." Paige slid her arm around his waist, smiled as a good morning kiss landed on her forehead.

"You were quite occupied with the counter display," Jake teased. "Doing inventory, maybe? Memorizing future selections?"

Judy leaned forward and whispered. "There actually is a line behind you two…"

"Oh, sorry!" Paige exclaimed. She smiled apologetically at the customer behind Jake and turned back to Judy. "I'll have a vanilla latte. And…" She looked at Jake.

"Black coffee," Jake said. He handed payment to Judy before Paige could reach into her purse.

Judy made change quickly and nodded toward the back corner. "The booth just opened up. You two should grab it. We'll call your names when the drinks are ready."

Paige took Jake's hand and led him to the booth, sliding in first and leaning forward, elbows on the table, chin resting on her hands. She surveyed the room, enchanted.

"You're like a schoolgirl on a field trip, Paige," Jake said as he rested casually against the cushioned back of the booth.

"That's what it feels like." Paige jumped up again at the sound of their names. Retrieving their drinks from one of the young helpers at a side counter, she returned quickly and settled in. She handed Jake his coffee, and then brought her latte up close to her nose, breathing in the sweet aroma of vanilla. She closed her eyes and sighed. The sounds of the busy café enveloped her – the buzz of the espresso machine, the opening and closing of the front door, light chatter among other customers, greetings between locals joining the growing line at the counter, change clattering into a tip jar, Jake's voice...

"Paige?"

"Oh," Paige said, opening her eyes. "Sorry, what were you saying? I got lost in the café's atmosphere for a minute."

"So I noticed." Jake laughed.

"I love the energy in this place, you know?" Paige sipped her latte, looked around at the activity. "I noticed the 'Help Wanted' sign in the window."

"You'll see a lot of those signs around town," Jake said. "Staffing is a constant problem in Jackson Hole. Tourists far outnumber the available workforce. And housing is scarce, which makes it hard to attract workers. You're lucky to have that cabin on Dan's property." He grinned. "Otherwise you'd be stuck living at the ranch."

"Funny," Paige said, not buying the bait. Besides she knew Jake was teasing. He'd understood her desire to get settled on her own before committing further to what they both knew would be a lasting relationship. "But that sign...it intrigues me."

Jake raised his eyebrows. "Uh oh, should I be afraid to ask what's going on in that pretty head of yours?"

"Of course not," Paige said, tumbling around the thoughts in her mind. "But ... what would you think about me helping Judy out here a few mornings each week?"

Jake almost choked on his coffee. "You're serious?" He set down his cup and wiped the back of his hand across his mouth. "You just left a high pressure job in a high pressure city. I'd think you'd want to relax."

"I do," Paige said. "But this couldn't be that much pressure..." The sound of the espresso machine pierced the air again. "Or it would be a completely different kind of happy pressure. It does look like Judy could use another barista or any kind of help."

Jake waved at an acquaintance who joined the line of customers waiting to order. "I'm sure that's true. Then again, what about helping me at the ranch?"

"Oh, I think you're in capable hands there," Paige said, immediately regretting her choice of words. Before Jake could pick up on the slip, she added, "You have a good team, a knowledgeable contractor, and, of course, I could help with anything later in the day."

"And pitch freelance articles, too?" Jake asked.

"Oh! Speaking of that, I have good news." Paige set her latte down. "I almost forgot to tell you. I emailed Susan last night about an article on the film history here. She'd already replied this morning. She thinks it's a great idea."

"She does, does she?" Jake laughed.

"What?" Paige paused. "Why, what do you think?"

"I think you want the job here for a discount on lattes, not to mention a few treats in that display case, and the article as an excuse to snoop into Percy Carter's interest in that *Shane* photograph."

"I'm shocked that you would think that!" Paige said, and then laughed. After all this time, of course Jake could guess her motives for her choices. Still, she chose her next words carefully. "I admit to the appeal of a discount here, but I honestly think the Hollywood-Jackson Hole connection would be interesting to readers, regardless of Percy Carter. You said yourself that you're a huge old western film buff. You surely don't think you're the only one."

"I can't argue with you there," Jake said. "You do know how to sniff out a good story. No wonder Susan was eager to keep you on as a freelancer." He finished his coffee and set the cup aside.

"Not going for a refill?" Paige always felt that to be an advantage of ordering regular coffee over a specialty drink.

Jake shook his head. "Not this morning. I need to get back to the ranch. I have a delivery coming in, and the electrician will be out to fix a short in Cabin 4."

"And I should get started on research for that article. I'm going to drop by the JH Historical Society and Museum and see what I can dig up."

Paige and Jake deposited their empty cups in the self-bus tub, and Paige walked Jake to the door.

"I'm going to stay and talk to Judy for a minute," Paige said.

"You just can't help yourself, can you?" Jake laughed. "How about a cozy dinner at the ranch tonight? I'll cook. Seven o'clock OK?"

"Sounds great," Paige said. She waved as Jake strolled off, his cowboy boots clicking against the pavement. Turning back, she approached the counter and waited until Judy was in between customers.

"Something sweet to take with you?" Judy asked, seeing Paige eyeing the counter display.

"Actually, no," Paige said, "as tempting as that sounds. I filled up on one of the blueberry muffins you were kind enough to have Dan bring me. But I was thinking about taking a job application with me. I saw your sign in the window. Maybe I could help out a few mornings."

"Let me think about that." Judy tapped a finger against her chin and looked up at the ceiling briefly, then looked back at Paige immediately. "How does six thirty tomorrow sound?"

"Perfect," Paige said.

CHAPTER SEVEN

The Jackson Hole Historical Society and Museum sat on Cache Street a block and a half north of the town square. Paige chose to walk to the museum, rather than attempting to find another parking spot. She passed art and photography galleries, shops featuring local products, and cafés offering a tantalizing variety of culinary choices. For a town steeped in Old West history, there was no shortage of shopping options or international cuisine. Now that she was here more permanently, Paige would have time to explore every inch of Jackson Hole.

Luck was on her side, as the historical society had just opened its doors. The man who greeted her was tall and unassuming. He wore a bolo tie and cowboy boots but bore himself like an easygoing professor offering office hours for students needing help or information. She needed both.

"Paige MacKenzie," she offered, extending her hand.

"Rob Stevens." He returned her handshake with a firm grip. "I heard you were coming to town. Figured you'd pop in here sooner, than later."

"Did you?" Paige said.

"Dan McElroy told me. He and I are both active in the Elks Lodge."

"I see," Paige said. She loved how connected people could be in small towns. "And you're exactly the man I hoped to see. Dan told *me* you know virtually everything there is to know about Jackson Hole's history."

"Let me give you a quick tour," Rob said, pointing toward a wall featuring historical photographs. A hallway beyond that led to more. She followed as Rob pointed out one exhibit after another: Mormon pioneers' homesteads situated along a stretch known as Mormon Row, early photos of the town square and valley, and artifacts from Shoshone tribes who inhabited the area long before pioneers came from the East. Paige found it all interesting, but had a particular focus in mind.

"I'm especially curious about the filming history in Jackson Hole," Paige said. "I understand quite a few films were shot here, including *Shane*."

"Ah, yes," Rob said. "We have many photos in our archives from various filming locations."

"I saw a few over at the Silver Dollar Bar yesterday," Paige said. "It's fascinating how many different films have been shot here."

"Well, the land is rugged and open," Rob said. "And the Tetons make a perfect mountain backdrop. We did have homesteaders here, and the landscape hasn't changed much since then, thanks to John D. Rockefeller Jr.'s efforts to set aside land for the national park. He bought up most of the land under the Snake River Land Company. He had to pressure Roosevelt to approve the additional land before the park was established as it is today. However, I will point out that the park evolved over a period of time. It was first declared a national park in 1929 in order to protect the mountains and lakes at the foot of the mountain range, and later had additional land named Grand Teton National

Monument in 1943. But today's Grand Teton National Park boundaries were established in 1950."

"Tell me more about the films that were shot here," Paige said.

"Glad to do that," Rob said. "I'm especially fond of that aspect of our history. Take *The Big Trail*, for example."

"The John Wayne film," Paige said.

"Yes, his debut film as a lead actor, in fact. He was just a youngster back then, only twenty-three years old. That movie was filmed in 1930. But it was hardly the first one filmed here. Silent black and white films were shot back in the 1920s." He lifted a pamphlet from a rack below the front counter. "Take this; it will give you a list of films shot here in Jackson Hole."

"Thank you," Paige said, taking the brochure. She opened it and skimmed the list. "I'm especially interested in the movie *Shane*," she said, thinking back to the photo of Alan Ladd and Jean Arthur that she'd seen at the Silver Dollar Bar. It was the photo Percy Carter had spent the most time inspecting.

Rob laughed in a kindly manner. "Of course. That's the one most people ask about. In particular, they want to go see the set. But I have to disappoint them. The town seen in the movie was built specifically for the film, out on Antelope Flats. It was later dismantled."

"I see," Paige said, disappointed. A visit to the site would have made an intriguing focal point for the article she'd proposed to Susan.

"There are still a few sites used in the film that you can visit, though," Rob added.

Paige's spirit lifted. "That could be helpful. I'm working on an article about Hollywood's connection to Jackson Hole."

"That's right, Dan told me you were a reporter back in New York," Rob said. "You're planning to keep that up? We have an excellent local paper here. Maybe they're hiring."

"I'm just planning to do freelance work for now, in particular articles about the Old West for a series the paper in New York has been running this past year." Paige paused as she heard the museum door open. She glanced over her shoulder as Rob eyed the entrance, and then looked back at Paige to continue the conversation. Paige was slower to turn back.

"Ms. MacKenzie?" Rob asked.

Paige turned back toward him. Had she imagined it? She felt certain she'd just seen Percy Carter enter. She glanced back again, but the entrance hall was empty. "Sorry," she apologized. "I just thought for a moment that I recognized the man who entered. And please, call me Paige."

"That's one of our new volunteers," Rob said. "He hasn't been in the area long. Like you and many others, he's interested in the film history here." Rob motioned toward the inside of the museum. "There's more to see."

Paige followed Rob, noting other exhibits she'd be interested in visiting later: the development of dude ranches, local history of Native American tribes, as well as geological and archaeology discoveries within the Greater Yellowstone Ecosystem. With Jackson Hole bordering Yellowstone, much of the history of the two areas overlapped.

"Feel free to take a look around while I go help our volunteer get started on a mailing we're doing."

"Thank you, I will," Paige said. Though tempted to follow Rob back to the volunteer area, she knew she had no reasonable excuse to do so, at least not one she could explain. Instead, she took in the exhibits, browsed the museum's gift shop, and then said goodbye to Rob, who was back at the front counter, on her way out.

As she walked to the town square, she saw that the shops and restaurants she'd passed on her way to the museum were beginning to fill with customers and lunch crowds. The traffic seemed to be picking up, a sign of the impending tourist season. The activity didn't distract her from her focus on what seemed to be odd coincidences regarding Percy Carter. Was it simply by chance that he arrived in Jackson Hole, obsessed over buying Jake's ranch, showed fixed interest in the *Shane* photo at the Silver Dollar Bar, and was now volunteering at the local museum, where film history was archived? She tossed these thoughts around in her mind, more and more convinced there had to be a connection. The question was: what was it?

Paige reached her car, started it up, and ran several errands while in town: signing up for a post office box – there was no mail delivery in Jackson – opening a bank account, and picking up groceries. Before heading back north, she filled up her gas tank. Now that she'd be working with Judy at the café, she'd be racking up more mileage than she'd anticipated. Her cabin was a good ten miles outside of town, Jake's ranch a few miles farther. She could expect a round trip of twenty to thirty miles daily. It would be smart to keep the tank filled.

She arrived back at the cabin to find Dan working outside the barn, his current project a creative burl tabletop with curved branches as legs. She pulled over to say hello, and walked over to the outdoor work area.

"What a great design for a table, Dan. I love it."

Dan grinned. "Why, thank you, city slicker." He paused. "I guess I can't call you that anymore, can I?" He scratched his head. "Then again, I think I can. It takes a long time to be considered a local here. Some would say you've got a couple decades to go. Others will ask which generation of your family homesteaded."

"A new bank account and post office box won't do it, huh?" Paige laughed, knowing full well that the distinction between local, transplant, and tourist was clear amongst old-timers.

"Not quite," Dan said. "But it's a start. I take it you've been in town today, getting organized. All set up for life here now?"

"Yes, maybe even more set up than I expected. I stopped by the Blue Sky Café and met Judy. I told her I'd help her out a few mornings." She noted Dan's expression lit up at the mention of Judy's name.

"Nice," Dan said as he sanded a corner of the burl tabletop. "She'll appreciate that. All the local businesses need help during summer months. You ever worked in a café before?"

"Not in a café," Paige admitted. "But I waited tables when I was in college. I can learn." She repeated the words to herself multiple times, momentarily wondering what she'd gotten herself into. But how hard could it be, serving coffee and baked goods to customers?

"What's Jake think of the idea?" Dan asked. Paige was certain she caught a glint of a smile in his eyes as he glanced up.

"Haven't told him yet," Paige said. "But it won't matter. He knows I'm independent. I hinted to him earlier that I might apply for the café job. Besides, he's busy with the ranch. And he has good help, very good help."

Something in Paige's voice must have given Dan pause, because he straightened up, crossed his arms, and looked at her, his head tilted sideways. "I don't detect a note of jealousy there, do I?"

"Of course not," Paige said quickly, and cleared her throat. Certainly Dan had seen Jake's model-worthy contractor. He had reason to think Paige might be jealous. She tried to shift the direction of the conversation. "Naturally, the ranch is going to take up most of Jake's time right now; that's only normal for a project that big. And I'm excited about the guest ranch opening. It's going to be fabulous. I'll be helping with some of the organizational aspects, too – bookkeeping, cabin décor, maybe even meals in the lodge. After all, I'll have more experience in food service by then."

"I see," Dan said, laughing. "You have a good point there."

"I thought so," Paige said. She grinned, said goodbye, and moved the car to her cabin at the back of the property. She sent a short text to Jake to let him know she was home.

She then unloaded the groceries from the car, put them away, set the new bank account's temporary checkbook on the kitchen table, and added the post office box key to her keychain. Then she finished hauling the few boxes she'd packed in her trunk for the drive west into the cabin and stacked them as neatly as she could in a corner of the back room. She'd take her time emptying them.

Checking her phone quickly, she saw Jake hadn't responded yet. This wasn't surprising; after all, he was busy working. True, he had grown used to using his cell phone over the past year and carried it with him everywhere now. He usually answered her texts right away. But he probably had workers running him in all directions, supplies being delivered, and paperwork to handle. Besides, she'd see him that night for the cozy dinner he'd suggested. She poured a glass of water and opened her laptop to work on the film article.

Jealous? She thought. *Absolutely ridiculous.*

CHAPTER EIGHT

Paige turned into the ranch driveway, relieved to see the trucks were gone and everything seemed calm. Only Jake's truck remained in front of the garage. She parked next to it and stepped out, a gust of wind sending her freshly brushed hair swirling around her head. So much for appearances, she thought. Still, she liked the outfit she'd worn. She'd set aside her usual jeans for a soft, flowing skirt in soothing blues and greens, matching it with a peasant-style white blouse that rested lightly just off her shoulders. The circular neckline formed a perfect frame for her necklace, a sweet locket Jake had given her shortly after she met him.

When she was halfway to the door, she heard scuffling. She looked back, certain the sound had come from somewhere near her car. Nothing was there, though she thought she might have seen the tip of a furry tail disappearing around a corner of the house. Wildlife was everywhere in Jackson Hole, so she knew what she almost saw could be anything from a ground squirrel to a coyote. In any case, there was nothing there now but wide open space and flowing wind.

Paige climbed the front steps and reached for the doorknob, then suddenly felt it would be presumptuous to walk right in. She ran her fingers through her hair to settle it, and then knocked.

Jake opened the door almost immediately, swept her into his arms, and kissed her in a way that told her he'd been eagerly waiting for her, which thrilled her.

"You didn't have to knock," he whispered, his mouth close to her ear. "The door is always unlocked, and you're welcome anytime." He loosened his arms and stepped back.

"That's a very tempting invitation, Mr. Norris," Paige teased.

"I certainly hope so." Jake grinned, and then motioned toward the dining area.

Paige looked over and gasped. "Jake! Where on earth did that come from?" A rustic table that could easily seat twenty people occupied the space where his usual dining set had been. She walked closer, inspecting the style of the massive oak piece. She ran her hand across the surface, admiring its smooth finish.

"I told you I had a delivery coming in," Jake said. "I want guests to be able to dine family style, all seated together, exchanging stories, that type of thing – if they want, of course. I have a few smaller tables coming in to scatter around."

"Smart," Paige said. "Some people will want to dine alone or have a romantic meal."

Jake pointed across the room. "Chris designed a small alcove to be built into that wall, just large enough for a table for two."

"Great idea," Paige said. *As long as it's not for the two of you.* She immediately brushed away the ridiculous thought. *Get a grip.* "You can set that aside as a reserved table when guests are celebrating birthdays, anniversaries, or other special occasions."

"Exactly," Jake said. "Speaking of special occasions, I believe this is our first dinner together since you arrived in Jackson, isn't it?"

"I believe you're right," Paige said. "And the alcove's not even built yet." She sighed dramatically.

"We'll have to make do." Jake laughed and headed for the kitchen, returning with a single red rose in a bud vase, which he placed near one end of the large oak table.

"How sweet," Paige said. She leaned over the table to breathe in the fragrant scent of the bloom, and then straightened up and smiled. "But I'm not sure the petals are large enough to hold whatever is creating the enticing aromas coming from your kitchen."

"True," Jake said. "Maybe you can help me there."

Paige followed Jake into the kitchen and pulled two plates from a cupboard, as well as eating utensils from a drawer. "Please tell me you have some kind of placemats. You'll want to protect that gorgeous finish on the new table."

"Two drawers down from the flatware." Jake motioned toward a lower drawer as he opened the oven door. A delectable scent of mixed spices wafted through the air as Paige turned back toward the dining room.

"Smells heavenly," Paige called over her shoulder as she set two places at one corner of the large table, moving the bud vase in front of the place settings.

"Pot roast," Jake called back. "My one and only specialty."

"I see," Paige said. "And what are we having with that?" She suspected this was the extent of the meal plan.

"Well, it has vegetables in it."

"That sounds promising." Paige smiled as she walked back into the kitchen.

"And I thought about making a salad…"

"Good thought," Paige said, a teasing tone to her voice. "Did that thought go as far as making one?"

"Almost," Jake said. "It went as far as picking up salad fixin's at the store. I put them in the fridge and then…" He spread his arms apart and shrugged, as if he had no idea what happened after that.

"Well, maybe I can help them jump into a bowl." Paige laughed. "What do you think?" She opened one cupboard, then two more before finding a bowl that would work.

"I think that's an excellent idea." Jake pulled the pot roast from the oven and set it on top of the stove while Paige put together a salad of mixed greens, cucumber, tomato and avocado, and found a bottle of Italian dressing in the fridge. Rounding up two wine glasses and a bottle of cabernet, they moved everything to the dining room and sat down at the table, pleased with the spread in front of them.

"Not bad teamwork," Jake said. "Thanks for pulling the rest of the meal together."

"We do make a good team," Paige said, holding up her wine glass as Jake filled it a respectable half way.

"Yes, we do." Jake poured an equal serving of wine into his glass and lifted it in a toast. "To teamwork."

"To teamwork," Paige repeated as they clinked their wine glasses.

With a few swift motions, Paige and Jake served the food. Jake's plate boasted a hearty portion of pot roast with a side serving of salad, while Paige's plate reflected the reverse.

"Tell me about your day," Paige said as she speared a wedge of tomato with her fork. She smiled before taking a bite, realizing how domestic she must sound. Even her words came out with a sing-song kind of lilt to them.

Jake smiled, as well, clearly thinking the same thing. "Just another day at the office, dear," he said. He popped a chunk of potato into his mouth and watched as Paige rolled her eyes.

"Seriously," Paige said.

"Actually," Jake said, loading up a mix of pot roast and carrot on his fork, "it was just another day at the ranch. This table was delivered, as you already know, and the electrician showed up and fixed the short in Cabin 4. Not much else happened around here. Oh, and I made pot roast." He grinned and held up his pot roast-laden fork like a trophy before downing the food. "How about you?"

Paige thought back over the day. "Come to think of it, I have a few things to report. My visit to the JH Historical Society was interesting…more than I expected it to be, in fact."

"That's good, right?" Jake said. "You found enough information for your article?"

"Some," Paige said. "But that wasn't the most interesting thing about the visit." She paused, watching Jake for a reaction. "I saw Percy Carter there."

Jake put his fork down, as if weighing his response. "Well," he said after a pause, "the museum is a public space. As long as the guy leaves me alone, I don't care where he hangs out: history museum, bars, or anywhere else." He picked his fork back up.

"I understand," Paige said. "It's just that something seems significant about the different places he keeps showing up."

"Significant in what way?"

Paige opened her mouth to answer, but before she could speak, Jake said, "No, wait. You're not going to start digging up a mystery where there isn't one, are you? How about just getting settled and putting the one article together for now? How does that sound?"

Boring, Paige thought. *It sounds boring.* She knew better than to say this aloud. Also, her curiosity was hounding her, and once the hounding began, she knew she wouldn't be able to stop investigating until she'd solved the mystery or learned that there *was* no mystery.

"I just think there might be a connection between the places he's showing up," Paige said. "First, he repeatedly shows up here on your ranch. Then he shows up in the hallway at the Silver Dollar, inspecting those photographs, especially that one from *Shane.* Then he turns up at the history museum – as a volunteer, by the way. Not just passing through for the morning."

"Hmm," Jake mumbled, his fork alternatively hovering over carrot, potato and meat. "I still don't see a connection. I have nothing to do with that Hollywood stuff."

"I'm not entirely sure about that." Paige set her plate aside, finished with the meal. "So many movies were filmed in this area. Maybe your ranch was used during filming."

"You think these old cabins were used in a movie? I'm sure I would know that. The realtor would have played that up when I was looking at the property because it's a great sales pitch." Jake shook his head. "No, Paige, this time I think you're off on a tangent that isn't going to lead anywhere. As for the guy pushing to buy the ranch, I think Carter's just the type of person who likes to get his way. It's over, anyway. I haven't seen him around here lately."

"You're probably right," Paige said. She watched as Jake took a last bite of pot roast, and then stood up. She picked up their plates and moved to the kitchen.

"Don't worry about cleaning up," Jake said, following her with the serving dishes from the table. "I'll do it later." He set the leftover pot roast and salad on the counter.

"Too late." Paige laughed and threw a kitchen towel at him. "You can dry."

"Yes, ma'am," Jake said.

Paige washed and passed each dish and utensil over to Jake, who obediently dried and put everything away. She handed one last spoon to him, covered the leftovers with plastic wrap, and then stretched her arms over her head. Jake took advantage of the move to pull her into an embrace.

"You sure you don't want a little more wine? Maybe stay and have a cozy night to go with the cozy evening?" Jake raised his eyebrows, his expression both innocent and full of mischief.

"Tempting as that sounds, I can't." Paige said. "I have an early morning." She kissed him quickly, opened the front door, and walked out to the driveway.

"An early morning?" Jake called from the doorway. "Anything in particular?"

"Just a little work," Paige opened the door to her car and grinned at Jake. "I forgot to mention it at dinner."

"Another freelance article already?" Jake guessed.

"Not exactly," Paige said slyly.

Jake leaned his hip against the door frame and crossed one leg over the other, thumbs stuffed in his pockets. "What precisely does 'not exactly' mean, Paige?"

Both Jake's sexy pose and the smirk on his face almost caused Paige to close the car door and head back into the ranch house, but she resisted. "I told Judy I would help her tomorrow morning at the Blue Sky Café."

Jake took no more than a second to understand the full meaning of Paige's statement. "Ah, so you did take that morning job."

"Yep," Paige quipped, tossing her hair over her shoulder as she slid into the driver's seat. She closed the door and stuck her head out the window. "Only a few mornings. It'll be an adventure."

"I'm sure it will." Jake laughed and shook his head from side to side. "Especially for Judy," he added.

"Very funny," Paige said, crinkling her nose.

"Maybe you can pick up a few pastry recipes that we could serve guests at the ranch when it opens," Jake suggested.

"Excellent idea," Paige said. "I'll work on that." She turned over the ignition, blew Jake a kiss, and drove off to her cabin.

CHAPTER NINE

The whirring sound of the espresso machine mixed with aromas of baked goods as Paige stepped inside the Blue Sky Café at 6:30 a.m. Although the sign with business hours indicated customers had to wait a half hour, Judy had blocked the door open so employees could enter.

"Good morning." Judy waved Paige in and handed her a full apron with a Blue Sky Café logo on the front. "You can put your personal belongings in the office." Paige followed a short hallway past a small kitchen, and deposited her jacket and bag in the back room. She slipped the apron over her neck, tied it behind her waist, and then stuffed her hands into two oversized pockets on the front, unsure what to do next. She checked to make sure her ponytail was secure.

"Put these in your pocket." Judy reached in the door with a pad of paper and pen. "We don't wait on tables, but it helps to be able to write orders down at the counter, especially complicated ones." Paige wondered how difficult café orders could be, but realized she'd always ordered the same latte and muffin or scone. She'd never looked closely at the menu, a simple chalkboard on the wall. But it was a small café; how complicated could it be?

Paige joined Judy in front, where one girl – an older teen, or perhaps a year or so into her twenties – was stocking supplies on the customer side of the front counter, filling wire racks with coffee cups, lids, creamers, sugar, and artificial sweeteners.

"This is Sara," Judy said. "She'll be helping out during her summer break from the university." Judy placed a hand on Paige's shoulder. "Sara, this is Paige. We'll have her a few mornings a week to help ease the load."

"Happy to meet you, Paige."

Paige bobbed her head, and Sara went back to organizing the display case.

"Let me show you the basic morning procedure," Judy said, leading Paige behind the counter. Judy opened the cash drawer, counted the beginning bank, and closed the drawer again. "We start with a specific amount of change in the morning, and balance it against sales at the end of the day," Judy explained. "Ideally, the amount at the end of the day equals the starting bank plus any cash sales taken in."

"What about credit cards?" Paige asked, pointing to a charge card terminal.

"Those tally separately." Judy said. "At the end of the day, the register will print out all sales, both cash and credit. The total printed out for credit should match the total on the credit card terminal. Don't worry about that; I take care of it in the evening. Just make sure to hit the appropriate "cash" or "credit" choice on the computer screen when you ring each sale in." She indicated the icons on the touch-screen monitor. "You'll be working mornings, but if you ever do end up closing, and the cash out doesn't balance, that's the first place to look: cash sales rung up as credit, or vice versa."

"Makes sense," Paige said, making a mental note to be careful when ringing up orders.

"Now," Judy said, motioning to a stack of white boxes. "These need to go into the display case. We bake some items, but some are from a local bakery, dropped off fresh each morning. Just put those out on trays. I've already made labels for each." Judy walked back to the kitchen while Paige arranged an assortment of croissants, scones, and muffins on serving trays and placed them inside the display case. As Paige finished filling the last tray, Judy returned with a plate of fresh cinnamon rolls. She placed one on a plate inside the display case, and set the rest on a back counter. "Don't worry, Paige. Just shadow Sara today."

"Shadow?" Paige repeated, though she suspected she knew what it meant.

"Just follow her," Judy said. "Be her shadow. You'll see how she rings up orders, how to box orders to go, what plates to serve inside orders on, all of that. Watch over her shoulder and jump in when she needs help. You'll pick it up quickly." Judy glanced at the clock. It was now ten minutes until opening. "Did you eat? Sara, get Paige something before we open." Again, Judy headed back to the kitchen. Sara, now finished with the front restocking and table setups, joined Paige behind the counter.

"We get a baked good and coffee drink when we arrive each morning," Sara said. She smiled as Paige's eyes lit up. "Yes, it's a nice perk of the job."

"You won't hear me complaining," Paige said. She chose an almond croissant from the back of a tray, but turned down coffee, both because she'd had some earlier at the cabin, and because the café was about to open.

Sara handed her a plate for the croissant.

"We try to keep our own food in the back office out of customers' sight," Sara said.

Paige made a quick trip to the back, took a bite of the croissant, and returned to the front just as Judy was flipping the "closed" sign to "open."

The line at the counter built slowly, just a few people at first, then a constant stream of customers. Paige watched as Sara filled the first dozen orders or so, gathering to go containers when needed, pouring regular coffee and observing the steps for more complicated coffee drinks.

"Blueberry scone and black coffee to go for Sheriff Parker," Sara called as she touched the corresponding sections of the touch screen. Paige grabbed a scone with tongs and slid it into a wax paper bag, then filled a cup with coffee, added a lid, and handed both across the counter to the sheriff, a sturdy man of about six feet. He seemed friendly though authoritative.

"We don't charge Wade," Judy called out. "He keeps us all safe around here." She pulled a cinnamon roll from a tray, dropped it into a bag, and handed it to the sheriff. "And you give this to that fine deputy of yours, Ernie Barnett. I know he loves those cinnamon rolls."

"Thank you, ma'am," the sheriff said and moved on.

"Earl Grey Tea and a toasted everything bagel – no butter – for here," Sara called. Paige sliced the bagel, dropped it in the toaster, and prepared the tea in an individual blue pottery teapot. When the golden brown bagel popped up, she put it onto a small plate and handed it to the waiting customer.

Time flew by. Judy ran other orders from the kitchen: bagel sandwiches, breakfast quiche with sides of fresh cut fruit, hot steel cut oats. Phone orders sent Paige digging repeatedly for the pen and pad of paper in her pocket.

"Paige, can you back up Sara for a minute?" Judy said as she brought two small orders of oatmeal out from the kitchen.

After topping off a hot chocolate with fresh whipped cream, Paige handed it to a waiting young teen, and moved to the register. "Thanks. I need a quick break," Sara whispered as she stepped away. "I'll be right back. Judy will help if you need to ring anything up."

"Thanks, Sara, I think I'll be OK," Paige said. As she looked up at the deep blue eyes of the first person in line, she suspected she'd been tricked by both Judy and Sara into taking over just then. Jake grinned as if he'd just pulled off a stealth maneuver.

"What may I get for you, sir?" Paige tried her best to maintain a serious professional manner, but found herself smiling anyhow.

"My order is pretty tricky," Jake said, tilting his head slightly to the side.

"Let me guess," Paige said. She closed her eyes and held one finger up in the air, as if the answer might be in a gust of wind. "Black coffee and black coffee."

"How did you ever know?" Jake laughed as he pulled a ten dollar bill from his pocket.

"I can read minds."

"Oh, really?" Jake leaned forward. "What am I thinking now?" he whispered, his voice low and alluring.

Paige leaned forward, matching his posture. "You're thinking that there are other people in line behind you, waiting to order," she whispered back. To confirm this, she glanced down the line, which angled off to her right, toward the front door. She grew suddenly serious because of who she saw. She kept her voice low as she looked back at Jake. "That Percy guy is in line, about four people behind you."

"Really," Jake said, clearly displeased. "He'd better not be following me. I've made my position more than clear."

"He might just be a regular customer," Paige suggested as she poured Jake's coffee and handed it to him. "It's a small town, and this is a popular café." She input the order into the computer screen, moving slowly to make sure she hit the correct icons. When the cash drawer opened, she handed him change for the ten.

"Thanks." Jake took the coffee and moved to a table. Paige noticed he was careful to not look down the line, but she took advantage of greeting the next customer to glance beyond. Seeing Percy's head swivel in Jake's direction, she had no doubt he knew Jake was there. Whether he was tailing Jake or simply there by coincidence, she had no way of knowing.

Sara returned to take over the register. Paige moved away, unsure if she was relieved or disappointed that she didn't get to take Percy's order. Another phone order kept her busy for several minutes. When she looked up again and surveyed the room, there was no sign of Percy. But a glance at Jake's table caused her to frown.

Thinking quickly, Paige approached Sara with a suggestion. "Why don't I make the rounds and refill cups for customers who are just drinking regular coffee?"

"Good idea," Judy said, having overheard. "It's quieting down now that the early morning rush is over. Sara and I can handle things back here."

Paige made a quick tour of the café, saving Jake's table for last. Finally, she approached it with what she hoped was a casual smile.

"Christine, nice to see you again," Paige said as she refilled Jake's cup. Had she not been holding a steaming hot pot of coffee, she might have been tempted to pat herself on the back for sounding so sincere. The attractive contractor was leaning casually forward, facing Jake. She had no food or drink that Paige could see, and no paperwork to go over. One hand rested on the table, suspiciously close to Jake's arm. A strong scent of perfume rose from the table, and Paige's eyes watered.

"Why, Paige!" Chris smiled as she straightened up and sat back in her chair. "I heard you took this little job."

Chris' tone reminded Paige of the condescending attitude some people had toward service workers. She stifled a sigh.

"Yes, I did," Paige said. "Judy really needed the help, and I have time right now. Besides, I can learn so much from working in a public place – about people, for one thing. Did you want some coffee? I could get you a cup."

"No, thanks," Chris said. "I just stopped by because I saw Jake's truck out front and wanted to go over a problem that came up this morning at the ranch."

"I see," Paige said. "What kind of problem…" She paused when she noticed the customer line was growing longer again. Sara was handing change to a customer while

Judy grabbed the phone. "Sorry, I need to get back to work." Adding a few drops of coffee to Jake's already full cup, she excused herself, and went back to the counter.

Two hours, eighteen phone orders, and forty-seven counter customers later, Paige sat down in the back office and kicked off her shoes. Although she'd only been at the café for four hours, it felt like ten. She pulled her share of pooled morning tips out of her pocket: thirty dollars. *Not bad*, she thought as she took a sip of iced caramel macchiato.

"Great job," Judy said, sticking her head in the door. "Same time tomorrow?

"See you then," Paige said.

CHAPTER TEN

Paige found Jake back by the horse corral when she arrived at the ranch mid-afternoon. The café work had been tiring enough that she'd fallen asleep at the cabin after showering and changing clothes. Once awake, curiosity got her thinking about the problem Chris had mentioned earlier. Had Percy been hanging around again?

Now, dressed in jeans and a clean T-shirt, she approached the corral, admiring the way Jake was casually tending to one of the horses inside the enclosure. His comfort level around the sizeable equines far exceeded hers.

"Looks like you survived the morning," Jake said as he leaned across the wooden corral fence and kissed Paige.

"Barely," Paige laughed. "It took a nap to recover. I told Judy I'd go back in tomorrow."

"Ah," Jake said. "So this is going to be a regular job."

"I only committed to three days each week," Paige said. "Just twelve hours total. Not quite what I'd call a regular job. But it was fun. And I'll get a free coffee drink and baked good each morning."

"*Now* I understand. There's the real motivation behind this." Jake laughed. "You'll do anything for a vanilla latte. Speaking of which, I plan to put in an espresso machine in the kitchen here. Seems like something guests would like."

"And I'll be an expert barista by then," Paige said. "I told you I'd come in handy." She rested her back against the fence and watched the busy construction crew. One man worked on a cabin roof, replacing old shingles. Another nailed down a new log on a section of buck rail fencing around the property line. Two other crew members were in the process of securing a large window, an addition to a second cabin. The window faced the Tetons and promised an outstanding view. Several others, including Chris, milled around the newest cabin, installing a hot tub on the deck. "Ooh, a hot tub!"

"Yep," Jake said. "Should be a good selling point for that cabin. We can charge a higher nightly rate for it, too."

"We may need to test it out," Paige suggested, her eyes full of mischief.

"That exact idea occurred to me." Jake laughed.

Paige yelped when she felt a large equine nose bury itself in her hair.

"Don't be afraid," Jake said. "She likes you."

"I'm not afraid. She just startled me. It's been awhile since I've ridden a horse, well, the last time I rode a horse I was with you, remember?"

"That's right. If I recall, you were less than an experienced horsewoman." He ran his palm down the horse's side and then patted her on her right haunch.

"Ha," Paige said. "Maybe you can give me riding lessons. What's this beautiful girl's name?"

"Butterscotch," Jake said. "'Scotch' for short."

"She's such a pretty brown color," Paige said. "And I love those spots on her back and hips."

"Her base coat is chestnut," Jake explained. "Appaloosa colorings can vary a lot. This girl has a blanket pattern with spots. Note the star on her forehead, and the snip by her nose."

Paige looked at the horse's nose and frowned.

"A snip is just a spot." Jake smiled, reading Paige's mind. "Just like the one on her forehead is called a star. It refers to location."

"What about that line on her nose? I don't suppose that's called a scratch, is it?"

"Nope," Jake said. "That's a stripe."

"Well, that makes more sense than 'snip.'"

Jake laughed. "Yes, I suppose it does."

"So, she has a ... star, stripe, and snip, right?" Paige tilted her head to the side and studied Butterscotch's face.

"Exactly," Jake said. "See, you're almost an expert now."

"Right," Paige said, a touch of sarcasm in her voice. She could see Jake fighting a grin. "What about those two, over there?" She pointed across the corral.

"Gunnar and Wildfire," Jake said. "Gunnar's the sorrel quarter horse, the one with red-brown coloring. Wildfire is the Arabian, the one with dark bay coloring: brown with black mane, legs and tail. I told you about him, feisty and high-spirited. He's settling down, though, getting more manageable."

"He's smaller than Gunnar, but looks taller at first," Paige observed.

"It's that long arched neck, plus his high tail carriage," Jake explained. "He knows how to strut his stuff, that's for sure. Gorgeous horse." Jake cupped his hand to the side of his mouth, as if the horse would be able to hear him from across the corral, and added. "And he knows it."

"I think it would be amazing to ride him someday," Paige said.

"I'll definitely give you lessons, but not on Wildfire," Jake said. "We'll take Gunnar and Scotch out when we go." Jake glanced at his wristwatch. He was one of the few people Paige knew who didn't check the time by pulling a cell phone out of his pocket. "Not today, though. There's too much to do here." He opened the corral gate, stepped outside, and closed it again. He moved close to Paige and kissed her cheek.

Paige and Jake walked back to the ranch house to find it empty and quiet, at least momentarily. Undoubtedly, workers would enter and exit with questions, but at least they'd have a few minutes to talk.

"Iced tea, by any chance?" Paige asked. "I could make some up."

"There's a full pitcher in the fridge," Jake said. "I think Chris made some this morning."

Paige hesitated. "This morning ..." She stopped herself. *Right*, she remembered. Chris had mentioned meeting the workers at the ranch before coming to the Blue Sky Café. Paige pulled the pitcher of iced tea from the top shelf of the refrigerator and poured two glasses. She replaced the pitcher, closed the door to the fridge, and carried the glasses out to the front room.

"You were saying something about this morning?" Jake said.

"Yes." Paige handed Jake one of the glasses of tea. "I was thinking ..." *Think quickly*, she told herself. "... about the conversation with Chris at the café this morning. She said there was a problem at the ranch?"

"Oh, that," Jake said. He thanked Paige for the tea, took a thirsty gulp, and then set the glass down on the dining room table as he took a seat. "Just some holes they found dug up around some of the cabins. It's happened a few times. I'm guessing it's just a fox looking for rodents. I've seen one around from time to time. Or it could be a coyote. Plenty of them in this area."

Paige sat down across from Jake. "Is it causing any damage?"

"No." Jake shook his head. "I told Chris to just tell the guys to fill the holes back in. The dirt's right there, next to the holes. The critter has managed to kick up some old, lost tin and aluminum, but as long as we collect that stuff, it shouldn't be a problem for guests. You've seen dogs dig for gophers before, right?"

"Not really," Paige said, thinking of her former Manhattan environment. "Well, maybe at summer camp when I was a kid. Sometimes the camp counselors had dogs."

Jake laughed. "You're such a city girl, you know."

"No reason to rub it in." Paige smiled and took a sip of iced tea.

"Anyway," Jake continued, "it's a non-problem. One of the guys filled the holes in. If the critter comes back, we'll just fill them in again."

"I don't think I've seen a fox before," Paige said, thinking back. "But I've seen a coyote. Scared the heck out of me."

"At summer camp?" Jake teased. "At a zoo?"

"No," Paige said, smacking his arm in jest. "Here in Jackson Hole, last year."

"Not surprising, plenty of them around here," Jake said. "Visitors often mistake them for wolves, but coyotes have a narrower snout and longer ears. They're smaller, too, more compact. If you saw them side by side, you'd know. A fox is even smaller, not difficult to identify."

"I'll take your word for it," Paige said. "I'd rather avoid run-ins with any wild canine, much less *all* of them."

"Jake?" Chris walked in, clipboard in one hand, pen in the other.

Paige watched as Chris approached. She had changed since the morning, and now wore a pair of cut-off denim shorts and pink tank top, which went well with her sturdy work boots, much to Paige's surprise. She'd tied a blue bandana around her head, her hair scrunched up in a topknot that had a casual, yet styled look. Paige found herself annoyed at how fashionable the haphazard outfit looked, a reaction that added to her annoyance. Why should she care what Chris wore to work? Of course, she knew the answer to that question: she suspected Chris was dressing more to catch Jake's attention than for the job. Almost as if to prove that very point to Paige, Chris leaned over the table to talk to Jake, exposing a more than an adequate amount of cleavage. Jake had the good sense to act as if he didn't notice, though Paige was certain his eyes flickered in the direction of the obvious display for just a second. Paige was beginning to understand how Jake must have felt about all the attention she'd received from Miguel, the beautiful handyman they'd met at a resort in New Mexico several months before.

"We're going to need to order more copper pipe. It'll up the plumbing budget." Chris set the clipboard in front of

Jake, moving closer to him, as if reviewing the calculated figures herself would help him read. "Or we could use PVC, if you want to keep the budget down."

Jake shook his head. "Copper will be better in the long run. It's worth it. I plan to keep this ranch for a long time."

"Good to hear that," Chris said. "Speaking of holding onto the ranch, I'm sure I saw Percy's truck around here last night."

"Really?" Jake said. "Right in front of the ranch?"

"No," Chris said. "Down the road a bit, around the bend, up by those old cabins."

"Was he in it? Or was it just parked there?" Jake leaned back in his chair, frowning. "And are you sure it was his truck?"

"It looked like his – dark blue, with California plates. Looked like the one he was driving when he came by that time he tried to get you to sell. And he was in it, at least I think it was him. Someone was," Chris said. "Looking over a large sheet of paper."

"A map?" Paige asked, trying to think what a large paper might possibly be.

Chris shrugged. "I don't know. It was almost dark. I enjoy short drives after work."

"You must wish you lived here year-round." Paige kept her voice light as she directed the question at Chris. "It's such a beautiful area," she added, hoping to cover her curiosity as to why Chris would specifically drive around Jake's area during off-work hours.

"I do wish I did." Chris smiled at Jake, a move so obvious Paige fought the urge to roll her eyes. "It's so peaceful up here, compared to my place over in Idaho Falls, being a city and all that."

Paige almost laughed, but stopped herself. She'd never been to Idaho Falls, but was certain it had nothing on Manhattan. "Yes, that's one of the reasons we love it," Paige said, reaching out to touch Jake's arm. *Two can play at this game,* she thought. Not that she needed to. She knew how Jake felt about her. It was the attractive contractor's persistence that made her want to stand her ground, just on principle.

Jake looked between Paige and Chris, as if picking up on the unspoken competition for the first time. Paige removed her hand from Jake's arm and checked her cell phone as an excuse to not look at Jake. She could feel the smirk without seeing it.

"Well, it's a free world and these are public roads," Jake said. "I can hardly control where Percy hangs out, whether it's in town at the local saloons, or parked around the bend. Unless he's on my property, I'm going to ignore him." He picked up the clipboard and handed it to Chris, boss to worker. "Order whatever copper you need. We're going to do this the best way."

"I agree," Chris said, as if the pipe decision had been partially hers. With a dejected look, she left the ranch house, letting the front door slam slightly on the way out.

"Well, that was interesting," Paige said, referring to the interaction with Chris without directly saying so.

"Not really," Jake said, missing Paige's intended implication. "I don't care what Percy does. He's staying off the ranch. That's all I care about."

"You don't think it's odd he would park close to here, looking at a map?"

"Not my concern," Jake said, standing up. "I have a guest ranch to get open."

"I understand," Paige said. She took both glasses, now empty, to the kitchen. Hearing the words come out of her mouth had confirmed her own interpretation: it *was* odd that the strange man would be parked nearby. Besides, the fact that he might have been reading a map piqued her curiosity, as well. What could Percy be looking for?

CHAPTER ELEVEN

Rob Stevens was ringing up a gift shop item when Paige entered the Historical Society. The customer was a woman in her sixties or seventies, accompanied by a young boy of about five. The child clapped and then reached out as Rob handed him a model of a covered wagon.

"Thanks, Grandma!" the boy said, beaming as he held up his new prized possession. "Look what I got!" he said to Paige. "The wheels turn. Cool, huh?"

"Very cool!" Paige said, mirroring the boy's excitement.

"You're welcome, dear," the grandmother said. "How about we go for ice cream next?"

"Ooh, yeah!"

The woman put her wallet away in a shoulder bag and escorted the boy out.

"Back to learn more about film history in the area?" Rob closed the cash register and put the merchant copy of the sales receipt in a pile with several others.

"I'm certainly hoping to," Paige said. "All I have so far is basic information – names of movies, the main stars in each, and other tidbits. Not enough for an article."

"You're most interested in *Shane*, if I recall."

"Yes, exactly," Paige said. "It seems to have the most appeal of all the movies filmed here, so I want to focus on it. Although I could use a few others in the introduction, come to think of it. What do you suggest?"

Rob reached below the register and pulled out a binder. "Here, take a look at this. You'll find still shots from the main films, along with dates."

Paige took the binder from Rob and looked around for a place to sit.

"I can't loan it out," Rob said. "But you can look through it in the conference room. That's where we have meetings, where the volunteers work, and where we do research. Make yourself at home." He nodded in a direction beyond the gift shop. Paige noted it was the same direction she'd seen Percy Carter head the last time she was there.

"Thank you, I'll do that."

Paige stepped aside as a family of four entered the building and approached Rob to pay admission to the museum. Clutching the binder, she followed a hallway next to the gift shop, finding the conference room Rob had described at the end of the hall.

It was a glorious place with floor to ceiling shelves full of the paraphernalia that held the secrets of Jackson Hole's past. Paige paused at the doorway and took a deep breath. The room smelled like paper and dust, a heavenly scent better than perfume, especially for someone like Paige who loved research so much. She set her things down at one end of the long rectangular table and pulled out a chair but didn't sit until she'd wandered the room's perimeter, fingers trailing along the books and notebooks. The shelves held carefully dated photo albums, history books on the area, memoirs by long-time locals, and story collections from original homesteaders. It was a reporter's paradise, a room filled with facts, dates, photos, personal stories and, undoubtedly, a few legends.

As she turned to go back to her spot at the table, she noticed a notebook, pen, books, and laptop at the opposite end of the table. This shouldn't have surprised her. Plenty of people were interested in Jackson Hole's history, she was sure. She paused at the stack, curious about the subject the other researcher was covering, but she had no excuse to pry.

The abundance of research material in the room was overwhelming, and Paige was grateful she had the single binder to use as a starting point. She settled into her chair and began. The black and white photos told stories both on and off the set. Some were still shots from the films, while others featured candid shots of cast, crew, and extras during free time: Kirk Douglas playing harmonica as Jim Deaken to Elizabeth Treatt's Teal Eye in the 1952 film, *The Big Sky*; Henry Fonda relaxing on set, accompanied by Margene Jensen, the local beauty he was dating during the filming of the 1963 movie, *Spencer's Mountain*; cast members from *Shane* hanging out after hours at the Silver Dollar Bar. They worked hard, they played hard, and they seemed to take advantage of Jackson Hole's opportunities for both.

After a few minutes of poring through the glossy pages and taking detailed notes, she started to drift into the past and felt the happy sort of tug she'd felt on her first visit to Jackson Hole when she encountered more history than she'd bargained for. She was in a daze of memory until someone else entered the room and sat at the table by the stack she'd noticed before.

It was natural for her to look up to see who was sharing her space.

Percy Carter. She took a sharp breath and hoped he didn't notice. He glared at her, sat down, and before she had a chance to say "hello," he flipped open his laptop and hid behind the screen.

Whether she was surprised or not to see Percy enter, she wasn't sure. She'd seen him the first time she stopped by the historical society, and Rob had said Percy was a volunteer, after all. But knowing Percy was the one reading that stack of materials fueled her curiosity. She wondered if his research had anything to do with his obsession with Jake's ranch, and if that obsession had anything to do with his interest in the photos he'd scrutinized so intensely in the hallway at the Silver Dollar Bar. Volunteering at the historical society gave him easy access to tons of information. Paige wanted to know what the connections were and what Percy was discovering as he read and took notes.

She went back to focusing on her own work, or pretending to focus, sneaking glances at Percy now and then as he worked. After thirty minutes or so, Percy stood and replaced something in one of the shelves. He zipped his laptop into a battered case, gathered his notebook and pens and started to leave the room. Paige kept her head down as he blew by, his speed rippling a page of her own notebook.

The door closed behind him.

"Whew!" she said aloud. "That man's energy could eat the rust off an old car."

She spun in her chair and looked at the closed door. A couple of feet from it, a piece of paper lay on the floor. She hadn't noticed it when she came in so she wondered if Percy had dropped it on his way out. She rose and picked up the paper, puzzled to see only a few phrases: town site, river crossing, and cattle herd. Next to each phrase was a set of numbers. She was tempted to slip the paper into her notebook, but thought better of it and decided to try to catch Percy so she could return the notes.

Rob looked up as Paige hurried past the gift shop where he was restocking books in a section devoted to the national parks.

"Is everything OK?" he asked.

"Yes. Well, the man who was in the conference room with me dropped this paper, I think. I was trying to catch him to return it."

"I can hold onto it for him for the next time he comes in to volunteer or do his research," Rob said. He took the paper from her and glanced at it. "Oh, hey, I think I know what these are. I'll bet Percy was reading through Walt Farmer's CD."

"Walt Farmer's CD?" Paige asked, confused.

"That's the likely place where he found this information," Rob said. "These are a few of the locations where *Shane* was filmed. Only place those are described in detail is in Walt Farmer's CD, *The Making of Shane*, which is part of his Wyoming film history CD."

"I see," Paige said, her interest growing. "Do you have a copy of that CD? Sounds like it would be helpful for my article."

"I'm sure it would, since you're interested in the film history here," Rob said. "It has everything you could ever want to know about *Shane,* and then some. We sell it in the gift shop, but there's one back there in the conference room. I'll make you a copy of this paper, and then show you where the CD is." Rob disappeared for a minute into the back and returned with a copy of Percy's notes.

Paige followed Rob to the conference room, where he became occupied searching a shelf toward the end of the room. Paige browsed other shelves casually, arriving at the one where Percy had returned an item. Sure enough, it was Walt Farmer's CD.

"Is this it?" Paige held up the case for Rob to see.

"Indeed," Rob said. "Wonder what it was doing over there. Our volunteers know to put things back in place."

Maybe not the new one, Paige thought. *Or one in a hurry to leave…*

"I'd love to borrow it, if that's allowed." Paige said. "In fact," she continued before Rob had a chance to answer, "I'll buy a copy from the gift shop. That way I can take my time and not worry about returning it immediately."

"I'm not one to turn down a sale," Rob said. "Every purchase helps support the museum."

"Then this will help both of us," Paige said. She gathered her belongings and walked back to the gift shop with Rob. She waited while he looked through a cupboard and pulled out a copy of the correct CD.

"Any chance of interviewing the author?" Paige asked.

Rob shook his head. "Unfortunately, he passed away a few years ago. But he tells the story from a personal viewpoint. You'll see when you read through it. It's also interactive, so you can follow links to additional information, like maps to the filming locations. Plenty of photos in there, too."

"Excellent," Paige said. "Not that he passed away, of course," she added quickly. "But wonderful that he included interactive links to photos and maps." She pulled out her wallet and paid for the CD. Excited to dive into the information, she thanked Rob and headed back to her cabin, taking the new purchase, as well as the copy of the paper Percy had dropped.

CHAPTER TWELVE

Paige joined Jake at his dining room table and pulled her laptop and Walt Farmer's CD out of her shoulder bag. Excited at the prospect of having a proverbial gold mine of information in her hands, she practically raced to the ranch after leaving the historical society, stopping at the cabin only long enough to pick up her laptop.

"Wait until you see the resource I found," Paige said as Jake sat beside her and handed her one of two glasses of white wine he'd just poured. "This has everything I'll need for the article on filming in Jackson Hole." *And maybe some insight into that weird Percy Carter*, she added silently.

"A CD?" Jake asked. "Western music to write by?" He picked up the plastic container and flipped it over, looking at both the back and the front.

"No, though that's not a bad idea. It's a book in CD form, a CD-ROM," Paige explained. "Interactive, so you can read it online and follow links to photos and maps, that sort of thing."

"Sounds interesting," Jake said, his tone showing only moderate enthusiasm.

"Interesting?" Paige repeated as she inserted the CD in the laptop. "Just 'interesting?' That's a word that rarely means 'interesting,' you know."

"Sorry," Jake said. "I'm always interested in your work. I'm just preoccupied with construction problems, including those darn holes that showed up. Turns out one is deeper than we thought, going down under the foundation. Chris thinks that crazy fox is building a den, and that it could be a problem for visitors. She's probably right. But living with wildlife comes with the territory here. I just wish we could encourage it to dig its den somewhere else, not under any of these cabins."

"Do you think she'll try to scare it off?"

"No, I don't think so," Jake said. "She might ask Wyoming Game and Fish to relocate it. But guests would love to catch a glimpse of it, if they could. Part of what brings people to this area is all the wildlife they get to see up close."

"I guess it's not as if you can get a doghouse and tell the fox to live there, instead." Paige pulled up the CD's table of contents.

"No." Jake laughed. "I don't think that would work. But, speaking of which..." His voice trailed off, causing Paige to look up at Jake, eyebrows raised.

"'Speaking of which,' you were saying?"

"I've been thinking this ranch isn't quite a ranch without a dog," Jake said.

"You're going to get a dog?" Paige paused to think this over. She'd never had a dog before, not growing up, and her busy life in Manhattan plus the frequent travel she did for *The Post* didn't allow for pet ownership. But she could see one fitting in on the ranch. "What if guests are allergic?"

"He wouldn't be allowed in the guest cabins, though I'd like a couple of them to be pet-friendly."

"'He?'" Paige repeated.

"Or she." Jake amended his statement. "It just depends on which one we choose."

"Ah, now it's 'we?'" Paige smiled.

"Of course," Jake said. "I'm not going to get a dog that you're not comfortable with. What if some day – hypothetically, of course – that wild streak of independence you have bends enough that you decide to live in, say, a nice ranch house rather than a small cabin. You'll want to be comfortable with whatever dog lives on the property, don't you think?"

"So where do you plan to find this dog?" Paige asked, smiling as she ignored yet another hint from Jake about her moving in. It had become a game by now between them, teasing about the possibility.

"A local shelter," Jake said. "We'll look around. Jackson has a great rescue organization called the Animal Adoption Center. That's where Dan got his dog. What do you say we stop by there sometime this week and see who's looking for a home?"

"Sounds good," Paige said, imagining a dog around the ranch could be nice. She took a sip of wine and turned her attention back to the laptop. "Look at this, Jake." She pointed to the table of contents.

Jake leaned in and scanned the list of chapters. "Lots of information there," he admitted. "Truly a reporter's dream, huh?"

"Absolutely," Paige said. "It lists movies filmed all over Wyoming, dates, cast information, production details – everything people could possibly want to know. Probably more than they'd want to know."

"More than you need for your article, that's for sure," Jake pointed out. "Aren't you planning to focus on *Shane*?"

"That's my plan," Paige said. "It seems to be the most popular of the movies filmed here, so it makes sense, though I'll add references to others." She didn't mention Percy's apparent preoccupation with the film. She debated whether or not to share the paper he'd dropped at the museum. In the end, she decided to show him. "Here, I want to show you something." She took out the paper, unfolded it, and set it on the table.

Jake picked up the wrinkled sheet and looked it over. "Coordinates," he said. "And look at these phrases – town site, river crossing, cattle herd. Where did you find this?"

"On the floor at the historical society. But this is just a copy. Rob Stevens, the museum director, made it for me." Paige said, leaving out the fact that she was pretty sure Percy had lost it when he left the conference room. "Rob said these coordinates refer to *Shane*."

"He's right," Jake said. "These are all locations in the movie. For example, the town site is where Grafton's is, not far from cemetery hill where they bury Torrey.

"Torrey?"

Jake laughed. "You need to see the movie, Paige."

"What about the river crossing and cattle herd?"

"Those refer to a couple of other scenes, one is probably where a herd of cattle is run through a homesteader's property," Jake explained. "The other must refer to Shane riding his horse across the Snake River, I'm sure."

Paige took the paper as Jake handed it back to her, thinking. "You're right. I need to see the movie. I'm curious where these areas are."

"Well, you do have the coordinates now, you know," Jake said. "You don't need the movie to see the spots."

"No, but I think I might need to see the physical locations used in the movie to see what he's looking for," Paige said, almost to herself.

"Paige?"

"What?" Paige looked up.

"To see what *who* is looking for?"

Focused on the paper, Paige had said more than she intended. She figured she might as well spill the rest. "Percy Carter. He wrote down the coordinates. At least I think he did."

Jake frowned. "First, I thought you said you found the paper on the floor at the historical society. And I have to tell you, I'm not crazy about you getting close to Percy Carter, research or not."

"That *is* where I found the paper," Paige said. "And I didn't choose to run into Percy Carter there. He was taking notes in the conference room and dropped one when he left. Naturally, I picked it up."

"Naturally." Jake's expression was a mixture of amusement, concern, and resignation, all rolled into one smirk. And a handsome smirk it was at that, Paige noted. She leaned over and kissed him.

"Buttering me up with kisses won't stop me from worrying about you," Jake pointed out.

"I know that," Paige said, sitting back. "But you really don't need to worry. I don't need to deal with Percy himself. But maybe his notes will give me an angle for the article. Maybe those locations have a special meaning."

"If they do, it's probably just to him," Jake said. "There are plenty of other locations in *Shane* besides those – Three Tree Hill, for example, or the Starrett homestead. Those are important locations in the story."

"Apparently not to him," Paige said, "or he would have listed those, instead." She paused, thinking this over. Why would he have more interest in some spots than others, especially those not as prominent in the movie? "Tell you what, why don't I dig into this CD and see what I can find, at least enough to sketch out some of the article outline for Susan, while you pick up a copy of *Shane* for us to watch later?" She refocused her attention on the laptop, clicking through the table of contents to the chapter detailing filming locations.

Jake brought a hand dramatically to his chest. "Why, I'm shocked you'd think a true western film buff wouldn't have a copy of *Shane* in his DVD collection."

"You have a copy already?" Paige looked up. "Great! How about the popcorn?"

"In the kitchen," Jake said.

"Perfect," Paige said. "Just let me read through this chapter on locations first. Then we can start the movie." *And maybe then I'll have a little more of an idea what I'm looking for.*

CHAPTER THIRTEEN

The line at The Blue Sky Café moved slowly and seemed never ending. Paige stifled a yawn as she handed a soy chai tea latte to a thirty-something tourist wearing a Yellowstone T-shirt and a pink cowboy hat that Paige recognized from a store window three doors down. It was the third such hat she'd seen since the café opened three hours earlier.

"Not much sleep last night, Paige?" Judy whispered as the woman walked away and a local teen approached the counter. Judy packaged up a cranberry-walnut muffin. "Your usual, right, Bobby?" Paige had already noticed that regular customers were creatures of habit.

"That movie, *Shane*? We watched it twice," Paige said. "I'd never seen it before."

"Ah, well it's about time you did, then," Judy said. "That's one of my favorites. Shot right here in Jackson Hole, you know. People ask about it all the time."

"That's what I'm told," Paige said. She paused to ring up a lemon-poppy-seed muffin, two almond croissants, and three blueberry scones for the next person in line, an office worker picking up an assortment of treats for the company break room. Sara boxed up the baked goods and handed them across the counter to the customer. Paige turned back to Judy. "I'm writing a piece for *The Manhattan Post* about the filming history here."

"Well, you sure can't leave *Shane* out," Judy said. "It's such a classic — cattle ranchers, homesteaders, a handsome hero riding in to defend a good family, a gunslinger personifying evil, an innocent little boy in the midst of violence. It paints a picture of the Old West. It has it all."

"And the scenery!" Paige added between an order of hot chocolate and another for a bagel sandwich. "I was reading about the filming methods yesterday. The movie introduced a wider format than had been used before, as well as being in color. It won an Academy Award for cinematography."

"It sounds like you two lovely ladies are talking about *Shane*." Paige and Judy looked across the counter to find Dan on the other side, his wallet in hand. He was the last one in line at this point.

"Yep," Paige said. "I just saw it for the first time last night. And the second time, as well."

"Well, it's about time," Dan said.

"Exactly what I told her," Judy said, already pouring a cup of coffee for Dan. "Two sugars, no cream," she added as she set the steaming beverage on the counter.

"Thanks, Judy." Dan picked up the coffee carefully. "I'm going to hang out and read the *Daily* over there, see what's going on around town." He pointed to an empty table by the window. "How about having a cup of coffee with me, Judy?"

"You should go ahead and join him," Paige said. "It's quiet enough that Sara and I can handle it. There's not even a line right now."

"I ... well, come to think of it, a break might be a nice luxury," Judy said, "now that I have both of you girls to help."

"There you go," Dan said, grinning like a schoolboy. "Make up one of those fancy coffee drinks and come over to the table." He grabbed a copy of the daily paper from a rack and walked across the room, taking a seat.

Judy looked at Paige and Sara and laughed. "After this morning? Running ragged like we've been? A hot drink is the last thing I want. But a tall glass of ice water sounds heavenly."

"One ice water coming up," Paige said. She poured a glass of water for Judy, scooped ice into it, and shooed her over to the table Dan had chosen.

"Those two make a cute couple," Sara said.

"I couldn't agree more," Paige said. "I swear Dan blushes when he talks about her. Says she makes a mean peach pie."

"She does," Sara said. "And it's not even something we serve here. She makes it up just for him. I think romance is in the air."

"Sounds like it." Paige watched Judy and Dan perusing the paper, laughing and commenting on what they were reading.

Customers kept Paige busy for the next fifteen minutes. She handled the line inside while Sara took and filled a few orders from the outside window to the patio. People often chose to sit outside on sunny days.

Paige grabbed a pot of freshly brewed coffee and called over to Sara. "I'm going to cruise around and offer refills. You OK for a few minutes?"

"Absolutely," Sara nodded, encouraging her to go. "The line at the patio order counter is gone. Even that cranky old guy has his coffee now."

Paige glanced through the patio window, spotting Percy Carter at a far table, his back to the other diners, coffee in one hand, phone pressed to his ear with the other.

"Sounds good," Paige said. "I'll make the rounds outside and inside."

"Excellent," Sara said. She moved to the register as a customer approached and pointed to a chocolate croissant.

Paige stepped out the front door, standing aside to hold the door open with her free hand as a young couple entered. She then walked around the side of the building and up three weathered railroad tie steps that led to the patio. She circled the area quietly, refilling a few coffee cups along the way. She passed behind Percy's chair, hesitant to interrupt his phone conversation. She could see over his shoulder. His coffee appeared untouched. As she turned away, she couldn't help but pause at a sharp response he made. "No, Pop, I haven't found it yet! You have to know this could be downright impossible." She stepped away quietly.

Back inside, she continued refilling coffee for those who wanted more.

"Did you see this article in *The Daily*?" Dan asked as Paige stopped by the table where he and Judy were sitting.

Paige shook her head. "I haven't had a chance to look at today's paper yet. I barely made it in here at six thirty to help Judy set up, and we've had a line at the counter since we opened."

"Look at this." Dan turned the paper so Paige could read it and pointed to an article halfway down a page. The headline read, "Holes in the Hole."

Paige repeated the headline, and leaned in closer, noting the photo that accompanied the article. She straightened back up. "I'd like to read it later. I'll pick up a copy on my way home."

"I'll leave this one on your cabin porch," Dan said. "Seems they've been finding some spots dug up out on Antelope Flats."

"Really?" Paige had stepped away from the table, but now turned back.

"Yep," Dan said. "Sounds a lot like the holes Jake was describing to me the other day, the ones on his property. Not too deep, some with dirt kicked back in. Fox holes, he said."

"Huh. You're right. That's about what his look like." Paige ran the similarities through her mind. Aside from the large hole under one cabin, the others were of varying depths.

Judy excused herself to answer a phone call, but motioned for Paige to continue talking to Dan.

"Any metal objects nearby?" Paige asked.

Dan shrugged his shoulders. "Doesn't say. The article just indicates it might be vandalism. Some sagebrush was pulled out. What kind of metal objects do you mean?"

"Just stuff that might have gotten buried years ago, things like tin cans or camping utensils. Jake's construction crew found a few items like that around the yard by some holes they think a fox is digging." Paige glanced at the counter to see a line forming again. Judy was off the phone and back at the register. Sara carried a batch of fresh cinnamon rolls from the kitchen. "I need to get back to work. I'll read the story later. Thanks, Dan."

Judy had just finished wrapping three warm spinach-feta croissants to go when Paige stepped behind the counter. The customer, a slender woman wearing a beaded rayon dress in a soft plum shade, added cups of fresh fruit to the order, and placed everything in a recyclable bag with a Jackson Hole Farmer's Market logo on it. Paige rang up the order, gave the woman her change, and wished her a good day.

One by one, customers came and went, until the line dissipated into a late morning lull. Judy's lunch helper arrived, and Paige retired to the back office with an iced coffee and almond scone. Like the day before, she kicked off her shoes to enjoy a few moments to herself. A copy of *The Daily* was on the table. She picked it up, turned to the article Dan had pointed out, and scanned it. As she'd suspected, the holes up in Antelope Flats did sound similar to those on Jake's ranch. The general area described in the article sounded familiar, as well. Unsure why, she read the story a second time before realizing there were similarities between the location described in the paper and that described in Walt Farmer's CD. Was someone searching for *Shane* souvenirs?

She was tempted to call Jake, but she decided not to interrupt his work. She'd see him soon enough. Besides, it was possible there was no connection at all between the digging on Antelope Flats and that on his property.

"Thanks for your help today," Judy said, sticking her head in the door. "I should be fine the next two mornings, but how's your schedule after that? I could use your help the following morning."

"Wide open," Paige said. "Then I'll be here at six thirty that morning. I may stop in for a latte between now and then."

"It's on the house if you do. I'm just grateful for your help." Judy ducked out as quickly as she'd popped in.

Paige finished the iced coffee and half the scone, wrapping the other half to go. She slipped her shoes back on, and hung her apron on a wall hook. Taking the newspaper with her —after all, a full rack of them sat by the entrance — she walked back to the front of the cafe, said goodbye, and stepped outside. She tucked the paper under her arm and started toward her car, a single thought running through her head:

Percy Carter is searching for something. But, what? And why?

CHAPTER FOURTEEN

Paige drove straight home after leaving the café. She waved to Dan as she turned into the property, but continued to the cabin and parked. As promised, Dan had left his copy of *The Daily* on the porch. She grabbed it, hurried inside, and set it and the copy she'd taken from the café on the kitchen table. It took all of five minutes for her to change to jeans and a T-shirt and fire up her laptop. She pulled Walt Farmer's CD out of its case and inserted it in the laptop. Scanning the table of contents, she clicked forward to the section devoted to filming locations. She'd read a few descriptions the evening before, but she hadn't had time to absorb much. And although she had coordinates from Percy's notes, the newspaper only described the site locations generally.

Antelope Flats was not far from Dan's property. Paige had been there before. It was a part of Grand Teton National Park known mostly for Mormon Row, an original homestead area where visitors could find the picturesque and oft-photographed Moulton Barn, as well as herds of bison and pronghorn. She could reach it by driving east past Kelly, following the road as it curved northbound, and continuing on.

The problem was getting to the exact area where she could find the holes from the paper's story. Paige had a hunch the holes were somewhere around the filming locations Walt Farmer had described. If she was right, she could find them by following the CD's description. It would take more than a car ride up the Gros Ventre Road, however.

Research she'd already done had clearly described changes in Jackson Hole roadways. The main highway hadn't been built yet when movies were being filmed back in the 1950s. Multiple dirt roads used at that time had since disappeared, overgrown with sagebrush. She'd need good hiking shoes and bottled water to make the trek.

Paige wrote down directions on a notepad and put it away. She grabbed her most comfortable shoes, sunscreen, and a baseball cap, filled a water bottle, and headed out.

The drive was a favorite of Paige's and not only because it took her toward Jake's ranch. It was far enough out of town to not be crowded with other cars, and the scenery was outstanding. Bison grazed in fields on both sides of the road. As Paige turned north after passing Kelly, the Tetons formed an exquisite backdrop to the landscape on her left, while a small cluster of pronghorn gathered to the right.

Paige passed the turnoff she would normally take to get to Jake's, a road that ran eastbound past Kelly Warm Springs. Although she was tempted to stop by and fill him in on her suspicions about the holes in the morning paper's article, she wanted to see for herself first. And if she didn't stop to share her plans, Jake wouldn't have the chance to tell her not to go off exploring on her own.

Pulling over several times to double check her written notes, she finally reached what appeared to be the right destination to park the car and start off on foot. She applied sunscreen and adjusted her baseball cap to shade her face. Attaching her water bottle to a loop on her jeans, she began the hike.

As Walt Farmer described in the CD, there wasn't a set trail directly from the road, nor were there any signs offering written directions. She used the angle of the Teton views, combined with tree and bush locations, to find the trail. Once on it, she followed similar landscape clues until she arrived at what she believed to be the old town site used in *Shane*. As she already knew, no structures remained. But now that she'd seen the movie, she could visualize the scene as it must have been during filming: Grafton's in front of her, with other wooden storefronts extending to both sides, the mountains as a backdrop, the dust beneath her feet as the road stretched through the rustic town. She could almost imagine Jack Palance stepping out onto the boardwalk, dressed in black, hand on his holster, eyeing her with an evil grin. She shuddered and turned away.

Inspecting nearby areas, nothing struck her as unusual. She searched in multiple directions, but found the ground undisturbed. Indian paintbrush and larkspur dotted the sagebrush-covered earth. All foliage rested comfortably beneath the warm sun, not a leaf or petal out of place.

Paige continued to study the area for the good part of an hour but saw nothing interesting. She rested on a cement block and took several gulps of water. She chastised herself for what now felt like a ridiculous hunch and wasted afternoon. Obviously the newspaper had been referring to a different place, maybe closer to Mormon Row itself, or farther west, by the highway. On the other hand, she felt certain she'd located the old town site for *Shane*, which could be an advantage for her *Manhattan Post* article. So perhaps the time spent had not been fruitless, after all.

After she took a picture of the area with her phone, Paige started back toward her car, detouring from the trail slightly in order to check other areas. She surveyed the ground as she walked, noting the same landscape coverage she'd already seen. Finally, after she took another water break, a glint of sunlight reflecting off an object about twenty yards to her right caught her attention. She capped her water bottle and walked over, her hopes growing as she got closer.

The glint of light had come from a metal object, an old tin can. But there was no hole beside it or anywhere around that Paige could see. She walked out twenty feet in one direction, and then began a circle. Just as she hit the halfway mark, she stopped and bent down, inspecting a rough patch in the ground. When she poked it with a stick, the dirt shifted easily, indicating it had recently been disturbed. Using that spot as a central point, she walked out another twenty feet, finding another, similar, area. This hole hadn't been filled back in, and a metal spoon rested a few feet away.

She kept searching and discovered more holes, usually with some type of metal object nearby. Paige took pictures of each location, remembering park regulations against removing anything. She did gather a few rusty items that might pose a danger to wildlife or visitors, but left the rest. Tempting as it was to retrieve all the objects, photos would have to do for most. Besides, Paige already knew what the items had in common: they were metal. She suspected this meant someone was using a metal detector to look for something in particular, abandoning anything that didn't turn out to be what they wanted.

Retracing her path, Paige returned to her car and headed for Jake's, eager to compare the photos she'd just taken with the holes on the ranch. Hopefully Chris hadn't had them filled in, at least not the ones outside the immediate construction areas. Before she started the car, she sent Jake a text to let him know she was on her way.

Moving along at a steady pace, Paige slowed as she approached the turnoff to Jake's place. A herd of bison that had been grazing at a distance when she was driving to the site for her search had moved close to the road. One particularly large creature stepped onto the shoulder. Paige slowed even further, finally coming to a complete stop as the bison stepped into the roadway. She checked her phone while she waited for him to cross. There was no text back from Jake, not that she expected one. He'd be occupied with business, or tending to the horses.

Paige looked back up, ready to drive forward. But instead of an open roadway in front of her, there was only dark brown fur, and plenty of it. In addition, a huge brown eye on a slightly tilted head stared at her through the windshield. The bison had chosen not to cross the road completely, but rather to take a break halfway across. In addition, to Paige's dismay, several others were in the process of joining him. In a matter of minutes, the entire roadway was blocked. She considered backing up and driving the long way back around Antelope Flats, passing Mormon Row and taking the main highway south. But a glance in her rear view mirror ruled that idea out. Yet another bison had entered the roadway. She was now surrounded.

Deciding this called for more than a text, Paige punched in Jake's phone number. While she listened to the ring, she sat up straight, trying to assume an authoritative position so that the bison directly in front of the car might interpret as her being in charge and move off the road. The huge mammal simply stared back. She could almost swear it tilted its head even more, mocking her.

Jake answered the phone on the fourth ring, to Paige's immense relief. He started laughing after her short explanation of her situation.

"How can you laugh?" Paige exclaimed. "I'm surrounded by these gargantuan creatures!"

"They aren't going to hurt you," Jake said. "Just stay in the car and be patient."

Paige sighed. "How long?"

Jake's voice faded as he answered a question from someone near him, a voice Paige perceived as distinctly female. *Chris.* "How long what?" Jake said as he turned his attention back to Paige.

"When will they move out of the way?" Paige's exasperation showed in her tone.

Again Jake laughed. "Whenever they want, Paige. They'll move when they decide to. I was in a buffalo jam once for an hour before they moseyed on."

"That's not reassuring in the least," Paige said. "And the one right in front of me is about the size of a battleship."

"Sorry," Jake said. "He probably weighs a good 2,000 pounds. I wouldn't try to take him on, Paige. I'm guessing he's got about a 1,900 pound advantage over you. Not good odds."

"Very funny." Paige sighed.

The female voice interrupted the conversation again. What was it with this woman? Wasn't a contractor's job to get the work done without bothering the employer every thirty seconds?

"Where are you, anyway?" Jake asked when he returned to her phone call.

"Out by Antelope Flats. On my way to your place, or so I thought."

"What're you doing out there?" Jake asked. "Didn't you work at the café this morning? And then you were going to work on the article for Susan."

"I did work this morning," Paige said, "but I wanted to check something out that I read in *The Daily*."

"'In *The Daily*...'" Jake was smiling; Paige could hear it in his voice. "You sound like a local already. What were you checking out? Or should I be afraid to ask?"

"Something interesting," Paige said. "I'll tell you about it if I ever get there."

"Just be patient," Jake said. "And drive slowly when you pass, after the bison move."

"Whenever that may be," Paige said. She ended the call and slumped down in the driver's seat, resigned to spending time with her new, unexpected companions.

CHAPTER FIFTEEN

"Thirty minutes." Paige sighed as she sat down at Jake's dining room table. "That's one forty-eighth of my day."

"It could have been worse," Jake said as he sat across from her. "I told you I was stuck for an hour once. That was up in Yellowstone, in Hayden Valley, on the east side of the park. Not uncommon there."

"Remind me to go through the west side if I'm ever in a hurry," Paige said.

"I'll try to remember." Jake laughed. "What were you out there looking for, anyway?"

"This," Paige said. She pulled up one of the photos on her cell phone and pushed it across the table for Jake to see.

"A tin can?"

"Not just a tin can." Paige took the phone back, flipped to another photo, and gave the phone back to Jake.

Jake frowned, looking at the picture. "I don't know what you're trying to show me, but I think your phone is sliding to photos you've taken before, Paige. Isn't this one of the holes in the yard? When did you take this, anyway?"

"You just proved the point I was getting to," Paige said. "This is *not* one of the holes here on the ranch. I haven't had a chance to take pictures of *our* holes. This one is out on Antelope Flats. Look at some of the other photos."

Jake followed Paige's directions and flipped from one photo to the next. "Hole … metal cup …hole …hole … old belt buckle …Honestly, Paige, I still don't know what you're trying to show me."

"They look like the holes you're finding on your property," Paige pointed out.

Jake shook his head. "Do you have any idea how many critters there are out here that dig holes? Coyotes, fox, marmots, ground squirrels – the list goes on and on. Remember, I explained this about our wildlife before."

"And they specifically dig up metal objects and discard them?" Paige asked.

"Well, no," Jake said. "But that could easily be a coincidence. Who knows what's buried out here? Decades – no, make that centuries – of stuff dropped by everyone from fur traders in the 1800s up to modern tourists. I really think your inner investigative reporter is on overdrive this time."

"Fine," Paige said, annoyed. "Mind if I walk around the property here? Maybe you're right. If I see the holes here, I might realize I'm exaggerating things." *Or maybe I'll find out I'm right…*

"Be my guest," Jake said. He stood up, moved around behind Paige, rested his hands on her shoulders, and kissed the top of her head. "Just be careful for loose boards and nails, that kind of thing. It is a construction zone, after all."

"Don't worry," Paige said. "If I can forge my way through a sagebrush forest and fight off a bison herd, I think I can manage a few wayward two by fours."

Jake laughed and leaned forward, whispering as his lips brushed against her ear. "Am I sensing a dramatic streak in you today?"

"Maybe a little," Paige admitted, her annoyance dissipating quickly. Jake knew her weak spots. It was impossible to stay upset with him when he turned on the charm.

The front door of the ranch house opened, interrupting what could easily have become a longer delay before Paige left to walk the property.

"Jake, could you help me with something?" Chris's voice was sweet and clear, with a seductive tone to it. "Oh, Paige, I didn't see you drive up," she added as she stepped in. Her speech now assumed more of a business tone. "We're finished with repairs in Cabin 4, and I just want Jake to approve everything."

"I'll be right there, Chris," Jake said as Chris stepped back outside. He turned back to Paige.

"Oh, Jake," Paige mimicked in a sing-sing voice, "could you help me with something?"

"Why, Paige MacKenzie!" Jake said. "That can't be jealousy I hear, can it?" He stepped to the side and looked at Paige, an amused yet somehow proud look on his face.

"Not at all," Paige said, realizing it was true as she said the words. She didn't doubt Jake's loyalty, and didn't see Chris as a threat. But it bugged her to see the way Chris hovered over Jake and played up to him. "I just think she should be able to work a little more … independently."

"First of all," Jake said, turning Paige to face him, "you have no reason to be jealous. She's not even my type."

"Really." Paige raised her eyebrows. "I didn't realize you have 'a type.'"

"Well, apparently I do." Jake laughed. "It's the overly inquisitive, trouble-seeking, stubborn, persistent, auburn-haired, green-eyed type."

"Watch it with that green-eyed part," Paige teased.

"You *do* have green eyes," Jake pointed out.

"True," Paige said. "But that's not the same as being a green-eyed type."

"I could switch the description to 'gorgeous-eyed type,' if that's better."

"Ah, I see," Paige said. "Now you're resorting to flattery."

"Whatever works," Jake said, a grin spreading ear to ear.

Paige stepped back and picked her phone up off the table. "What will work right now is letting me look at the holes on your ranch while you deal with the overly flirtatious, blonde, beauty queen, truly green-eyed type who is out there helplessly waiting for your rescue."

"Actually, her eyes are …"

"Don't even!" Paige snorted as she stepped out onto the front porch and headed onto the property. As much as she tried not to generalize male behavior, knowing what *not* to say in a conversation didn't always make the cut.

The beeping sound of a construction vehicle backing up mixed with worker chatter as Paige moved from one area to another, surveying the ground. Most holes had been filled in, as evidenced by dirt recently kicked around. But several remained open near a side fence, one inside the property line and several outside. Perhaps no one had discovered them since they weren't in the immediate construction area. Paige took photos, but even without pulling up the images she took at Antelope Flats, she could tell they were similar. She also found metal objects, as she now suspected she would: a crumpled chewing tobacco tin, a flat can opener, and a keychain with a silver-plated trout dangling from it. Some looked older than others, but the common link was metal on all or part of each item.

Paige took additional photos and returned to the ranch house, meandering between cabins on her way to look for additional holes. Chris had resumed her seductive manner by leaning against a cabin wall, one hip thrust out to the side while going over clipboard notes with Jake. Paige rolled her eyes and continued to the house.

Over a glass of iced tea, Paige studied the photos. She realized Jake had a point; there were many critters in the area that could be digging the holes. But she didn't buy it that the metal objects were coincidental. Yet if someone was digging for metal, why leave the items behind? In that case, it wasn't for the material, to melt it down or whatever else could be done with it. The only logical conclusion was that a person, not an animal, was searching for something specific. What was it? And had someone already found it?

Paige wrote a note to Jake telling him she'd be in her cabin working on the piece for Susan. The statement wasn't entirely false, although her curiosity about the metal objects currently exceeded her desire to work on the article. Still, she'd already been out to Antelope Flats. That certainly qualified as writing research since it was one of the *Shane* filming sites.

CHAPTER SIXTEEN

Settled in at her own cabin, Paige got to work on the article. Used to deadlines, she forced herself to concentrate on the historical details of filming in Jackson Hole. Hollywood had certainly made good use of the area for decades, giving her plenty of fascinating material to explore. Still, she felt something was lacking, something with more of a local flavor and maybe less focus on Hollywood.

Paige fixed a cup of coffee, and stepped out on the porch, her mind wandering. As hard as she tried to focus on the article, her thoughts kept returning to the piece in *The Daily*. Why would similar holes and objects be showing up in multiple locations?

Following a sudden hunch, Paige went back to her laptop, brought up her notes on filming spots for *Shane*, and studied the list she'd made of locations. Jake's property had definitely not been one of them. That shot down a growing theory that *Shane* locations were the only ones being searched. Or ... did it? What if the searches were both on and *around Shane* filming sites, not necessarily *on* them? This puzzled Paige even more. Why would that even be the case? None of it made sense as a whole, despite the tenuous ties.

Her thoughts reverted to the locations of the current digging, and she pulled out the note Percy had dropped at the historical center. There were three phrases jotted down alongside the coordinates. One, the "town site," corresponded with the area she had searched out on Antelope Flats. What about the other two? Could Percy be following the person doing the digging? Or could Percy be the one *doing* the digging? She'd already suspected that Percy was searching for something, but it was troubling to think – since there were holes on Jake's ranch as well as outside the fence – that Percy had trespassed on Jake's property even though Jake had warned him to stay away.

Paige had been out to the town site, but that left two other phrases on Percy's note: "river crossing" and "cattle herd." Neither made much sense, though Paige knew from the Walt Farmer CD and from Rob at the museum that these phrases and coordinates were related to *Shane*, just as the town site had been. Since she'd just seen the movie, she was well aware there were scenes with a river in it, as well as many with cattle. But they were all independent scenes. The river didn't run through the town. The cattle herds were on ranches, not in town. Any way she looked at it, she couldn't see a common thread between them, other than scene settings that fit the story, but in different sections.

Paige pulled up a map application, inputting the coordinates that accompanied the "river crossing" phrase. As she suspected, the location that came up was nowhere near the movie's town site at Antelope Flats. Instead, it was off to the west, alongside the Snake River. She thought about researching the third location, too, but her desire to find and study the second was too strong. She grabbed her car keys and left the cabin. One destination at a time.

A left turn from the driveway set her heading west, away from Kelly, and along the Gros Ventre River. Slowing down twice for whitetail deer in the road, Paige turned right five minutes later and drove north. The view of the Tetons towering to her left never ceased to amaze her. Clear, sunny skies accentuated the mountains' snow-capped peaks. It was no wonder the valley had been used for so many Hollywood projects. It was dramatic and expansive, almost surreal, as if in possession of a backdrop painted specifically for the films.

Passing the airport – notably the only airport located inside a national park – Paige continued north, beyond Moose Junction, one of two access points to the inner loop, a road that ran spectacularly close to the mountain range. She bypassed several other turnouts before taking a left at the one she suspected she wanted: Schwabacher Landing. This favorite spot for photographers and painters offered a mirror view of the Tetons along a bend in the Snake River. It seemed a promising spot for the only river crossing she could remember from watching the movie: a scene where Alan Ladd rides his horse across the water, Teton views in the background.

Paige followed the road, paved part of the way, yet unpaved as it approached the parking spaces at the end. She pulled into a spot, not surprised to see an artist with an easel by the water, paintbrush in hand. Neither was she surprised to see a bride and groom posing for wedding shots, their photographer changing positions with the ease of a dancer, capturing the happy couple's memories from multiple angles. It was a perfect scene for memorable photos.

Weather was on her side, as the clear skies and lack of wind afforded a dazzling reflection of the mountains in the water. She scouted the outskirts of the area near the river's bend. Although the painter stood far enough from the water's edge that Paige could have searched that area, she would have blocked the Snake River background for the photo shoot if she had approached. To kill time, she strolled down the trail that ran to the north, past trees and shrubs, and alongside the grassy river's edge. A log dam announced a beaver pond ahead. Sitting on a bench to give the wedding couple and photographer time to finish, she was rewarded with the sight of a bumpy head and stubby ears just ahead in the rippling water. The beaver swam away from her and into a den of built up branches and shrubs.

Paige stood, ready to head back along the path, but froze at the sound of rustling in nearby bushes. A sudden panic ran through her as she recalled a news article about a grizzly attack in the area years ago. She hadn't thought to bring bear spray with her, always advised, since she'd had no intention of hiking. She had a can in the car, but that was hundreds of yards back. Holding her breath, she stayed still and waited. What was the usual advice given by the park rangers? Don't run, just back away slowly, that was it. She inched back as the rustling continued. Finally, she exhaled when a marmot emerged from the bushes.

"You scared me! I've never been so relieved to see a critter in my life. I thought you were a bear!" The annoyed marmot scurried back into the bushes, and Paige continued back to the trailhead.

As she'd hoped, the wedding shoot was over, the happy couple climbing back into a car in the parking lot, the photographer into another. Paige noted the painter seated on a folding chair, taking a break. Now that she knew she wouldn't be in anyone's way, she approached the water's edge.

The area closer to the river was muddy, not dry. She surveyed the ground, discouraged. If anyone had been digging during recent days, the chance of holes remaining was slim. Even though the wind was calm now, the previous night's gusts could easily have caused the water to lap over any sign of activity. She stepped cautiously to the side, inspecting another area, but found the same thing: no sign of any disturbance along the river's edge. Yet another sidestep gave her a vantage point to see into the water, which is when she spotted a sparkling object below the water's edge. Estimating the distance at approximately a foot from the shoreline, she took a step closer, testing the ground, finding it solid. Even better, she was close enough to see more clearly. It was evident now that the object in question was some kind of metal.

Feeling confident, she took one more step, bringing her within reaching distance of the object, which is when, to her dismay, she felt her foot slip out from under her. Within seconds, she found herself sitting in shallow, muddy water, debris floating over her legs, mosquitoes bidding her arms a welcome. Contrary to her usual self-restraint, she muttered a few choice words and slapped the insects away from her skin.

"Are you all right?" The artist called over from her easel, where she had resumed painting while Paige was exploring the river's edge.

"I believe the only thing bruised is my ego," Paige shouted back as she stood up and brushed the muck off her body. She smiled at the woman to indicate she was fine, and then looked around, grateful to see she hadn't had any other audience. The photography group had departed, and no new arrivals had come down the trail. She waved to the painter and slopped her way back to the parking area, her shoes squishing every step of the way.

Aside from her own Subaru, only one truck and a few other vehicles dotted the lot, all with out-of-state plates. This was common in the area since visitors came from everywhere, and rental cars at the airport often came from nearby states. She unlocked her car, grabbed a towel from the back, and covered the driver's seat, hoping to keep her newly acquired collection of Snake River debris off the upholstery. She returned to the back of the car to close the hatchback and glanced around the lot, suddenly noticing one truck in particular, two spaces down from hers: dark blue, with California plates. Wasn't that the description Chris had given of the truck parked around the bend from Jake's place? It had to be Percy's.

Paige averted her eyes quickly as the driver's door of the truck opened, and a man stepped out. She rummaged in her trunk area in order to appear unaware of his presence, but shuddered as he started her way, growing more nervous the closer he walked. She relaxed slightly as he passed behind her and continued on across the lot to a rustic restroom. He stepped inside and closed the door.

Propelled by the curiosity that so frequently got her in trouble, Paige sauntered casually over to the truck, cell phone ready to use as a handy excuse if Percy emerged quickly. It would only take a second to face the Tetons and pose, as if taking a picture. She lifted her phone into position as she walked around the far side of his truck, head facing the mountains, eyes glancing sideways at the truck bed. A canvas tarp covered its lumpy contents.

Looking back across the parking lot, Paige could see the restroom door was still closed. She glanced again at the tarp, and then up at the restroom. Finally, leaning against the truck as if propping herself to stabilize the photo opportunity, she dropped her free arm inside the interior of the truck bed and casually lifted the edge of the tarp and appraised the variety of items it covered: a folded ladder, a red tool box ...

"Hey! What do you think you're doing?"

Paige jumped at the sound of the gruff voice. She looked up, seeing, as she feared, Percy running from the direction of the restroom. Even from a distance, she could see his face was red and his body language angry.

"I ... I'm so sorry," Paige shouted. Thinking quickly, she reached into the truck bed with her other arm, and then pulled both out, holding up her cell phone. "I'm such a klutz!" she exclaimed. "I just feel like an idiot." *Both true enough statements*, she thought, hearing the words come out of her mouth. "I was taking a picture with my phone and stepped back to frame the shot. I bumped into your truck and dropped my phone in. I'm so sorry!"

Her flimsy excuse seemed to work, as Percy slowed, and his facial expression relaxed. Still, his voice was terse as he approached. "Fine, then. But you might think about being more careful in the future." He paused and frowned, undoubtedly noticing Paige's muddied appearance, but said nothing about it.

"I certainly will." Paige's voice held a mix of relief and embarrassment. She apologized again, and started back to her car.

"Wait a minute," Percy called, causing Paige to flinch. "You look sort of familiar. Do I know you from somewhere?"

Paige paused and turned back to face Percy. She mentally crossed her fingers that he wouldn't remember seeing her in the museum's conference room. "I work at The Blue Sky Café," she said. *Yet another true statement.* "You might have seen me there."

Percy nodded. "That's probably it. Good coffee you have there."

"Thanks," she said.

To Paige's immense relief, he got in his truck, started up the engine, and drove off, a cloud of dust and gravel rising behind him.

Paige sat back against the driver's seat in her car, suddenly exhausted. She inhaled, and then exhaled several times, just to calm her nerves. Driving back to her cabin, she thought back to Percy's truck bed. Not much she'd seen had surprised her. Besides the ladder and tool box, there were some old rags, a sleeping bag, and a set of jumper cables – all things that might be found in any guy's truck. But one thing in particular stood out from the others. Unless she had imagined it, she was certain she'd seen a metal detector.

CHAPTER SEVENTEEN

"Let me guess ... mud wrestling?" Jake's smirk was not the first thing Paige expected to see when she returned to the cabin and stepped out of her car. She was always happy to see him, but would have welcomed a chance to jump in the shower and change clothes first.

"Do they have that around here?" Paige asked as she raked her fingers through her hair, sending several twigs to the ground in the process. "Maybe I'll take it up as a hobby."

"Only pig wrestling that I know of," Jake said. "But you can get mighty dirty doing that. They have it every year at the Teton County Fair in July."

"I'll think about it," Paige said, walking past Jake's casual stance on her front porch. She waved him in behind her and pulled a pitcher of iced tea out of the fridge, setting it on the counter. "Be right out," she said, grabbing a change of clothes and heading for the shower.

Ten minutes later, Paige emerged, hair dripping wet, but mud, twig, and grass free. Clean jeans and an old but freshly laundered T-shirt had never felt so luxurious. She took a seat at the kitchen table and propped her bare feet up on another chair.

"I came by on my way back from town. I had to pick up a couple things at the hardware store, and was thinking on the way back that we could go check out the dogs at the shelter tomorrow – that is, if you're not planning another aquatic adventure like this after work."

"Funny," Paige said. "No, a visit to the shelter definitely sounds more inviting than a repeat of this episode."

Jake slid a glass of iced tea across the table. "Here. I poured you a glass, too. Unless ... maybe you need something stronger? Like whiskey with a shot of common sense on the side?"

Paige shook her head and smiled. "Iced tea is fine. I just slipped and fell, that's all. No harm done."

"I see," Jake said. "I'm guessing this didn't happen at your cabin, which is where you were supposed to be, writing."

"Very perceptive of you," Paige said. "I was up at Schwabacher Landing."

"Ah, beautiful spot," Jake said. "Did you see the beaver pond? In fact, did you leave any twigs for the beavers? It looked like you brought quite a few back with you."

Paige smacked Jake's arm playfully. He caught her arm, pulled her into his lap, and buried his face in her neck. "Mmm ..." he sighed. "What is that? Lemon?"

"Lemongrass ginger shampoo, if you must know." Paige laughed as she extricated herself from his grasp and sat back in her chair. "Actually, I think I figured something out while I was up there."

"Aside from the fact that swimming with beavers might not rank up there with swimming with dolphins?"

"I'm not even going to comment on that, other than to say I did *not* fall in the beaver pond." Paige said. "But I've been forming a theory that I wanted to check out, which is why I went up there."

"Somehow I'm afraid to hear what's coming, but go ahead and tell me." Jake took a drink of iced tea and set the glass down.

"It's about Percy, about why he kept hanging around your place." Paige talked quickly, raising one hand to keep Jake from protesting as she continued. "He wasn't interested in your land itself. He was looking for something. He still is. And I think your ranch is just one of several areas he's been searching. I think he's the one who's been digging the holes in and around your property."

Jake sighed. "That's a little far-fetched, don't you think? It's pretty obvious that fox is doing the digging."

"Yes," Paige said. "As for that large hole under the cabin, I do think it's the fox digging a den. But not the smaller holes – those are being dug up by a person, and I think that person is Percy."

Jake remained silent while Paige continued to explain how she'd gone to check the holes at Antelope Flats when the newspaper's description matched the ones at Jake's. The trip to Schwabacher Landing was to see if there were other holes that were similar.

"I think I'm following, or at least I'm following the way your imaginative mind works," Jake said. "You're checking the locations on that paper you say Percy dropped, the one with the phrases from the movie."

"Yes," Paige said. "And I think the term you're looking for is 'investigative mind,' not 'imaginative mind.'"

"I'm not sure about that," Jake said.

"I will argue that it takes some degree of imagination to investigate." Paige drummed her fingers on the table as she waited for Jake to see the connection. He might think – well, he *did* think – that she had a tendency to head off on wild goose chases. However, there was a method to her sometimes unclear process, whether it seemed like it on the surface or not. Without imaginative trial and error, some puzzles simply wouldn't be solved. She knew that, just as she knew Jake would understand her better if her unconventional techniques of exploration made sense to him.

"OK, maybe a little of both, then." Jake admitted. "So you searched Schwabacher Landing because of the reference to a river crossing in the notes."

"Right," Paige said. "You thought that referred to Alan Ladd riding across the Snake River. What I've read says that's the correct location."

"I can see that after watching the film multiple times, plus I've visited the landing myself," Jake said. "It's the right view of the mountains behind. That section of the river can change from season to season, depending on the amount of snow and runoff. So it may not look exactly like it did in the movie. But you've probably got the right place."

"We should watch the movie again," Paige suggested.

"You won't get an argument from me on that," Jake said. "I could watch it a dozen more times. How about tonight? Bring in pizza? I have to run into town to check the mailbox at the post office, anyway. I'll pick one up."

"Deal, but no green peppers, spinach, or basil, OK?" Paige smiled her sweetest smile.

"Uh, sure, Paige. I'll just ask for the non-green pizza special," Jake said. "I'm sure it's a regular menu item. Anything else?"

"Add tomato, mushroom, and extra cheese?"

"No, I meant about what you found out today," Jake said. "It sounded like more than just discovering the unstable marsh section beside the river. How did you end up getting that close anyway?"

Paige ran over the chain of events in her mind, hoping to get them in an order Jake would see as connected. "You know the metal objects you've been finding on your property, right? Near those holes?"

"Sort of, but I don't see why you think they're connected to the holes. They aren't in them. In fact, many are a fair distance away."

"I think I know why now," Paige said. "I suspect Percy is searching for a particular object. When he finds the wrong item, he abandons it, or even tosses it off into the distance, maybe out of frustration at not finding whatever he's looking for."

Jake shook his head. "How would this supposed person even know where to look? And why metal? And why on earth do you think it is Percy now?"

"Well ..." Paige chose her words carefully, knowing she'd have to admit she searched the back of Percy's truck. There was no question this would not go over well. "It's like this ..."

"It's always scary when you begin a sentence like that." Jake folded his arms and sat back, waiting for more explanation.

Paige leaned forward, determined to counteract Jake's closed body language. Crossed arms rarely indicated an open mind. "Metal objects are the only similarity between the holes, aside from locations that may be connected to the movie. And it happens there was a truck in the parking lot at Schwabacher Landing when I returned to my car. It matched the description you and Chris have both given of Percy's vehicle."

"You didn't." Jake closed his eyes, waiting.

"I was parked right by him," Paige began.

"Right by him?"

"OK, a couple spaces down. But he went into the restroom, which gave me a chance to glance inside the truck bed."

"This just gets worse and worse, Paige," Jake said. "Don't tell me you took advantage of a man's call to nature to rummage around inside the truck. That's called ... gee, what's the word for that? *Illegal*, that's it. Tell me he didn't catch you. I don't think the guy's someone to mess with."

"He didn't see me at first," Paige said. "And all I did was peek under his tarp. I didn't disturb anything. But it's what I found that was important, as far as I'm concerned."

"What was under the tarp? My guess is work supplies," Jake said. "Let's see ... what do I keep in the back of my own truck? My tool box, some ropes, a ladder, a spare tire ..."

"OK, I get your point," Paige said. "Normal guy stuff, and some of that was there. But I bet you don't have a metal detector in the back of your truck."

Jake looked at Paige more attentively now. "He had a metal detector? That's sort of odd, I guess."

"It's not odd if he's trying to find something metal that he thinks is buried." Paige sat back, this time crossing her own arms in satisfaction, as if resting her case.

"Could be a coincidence."

"Just look at all the 'coincidences' then," Paige said. "Percy showed all that interest in the *Shane* photos, then volunteered at the historical society, then had Walt Farmer's CD out, and he wrote down coordinates for several locations connected to the film. Three of those have turned up some degree of digging, many with metal objects tossed aside."

"Indicating he's not finding anything of interest."

"Maybe not yet," Paige continued. "But I'm convinced he's looking for something connected with the film." Paige paused, thinking about this. "In fact, I wonder what his background is. Maybe he, or someone he knows, had something to do with the film, something he doesn't want found out."

"That's a stretch, Paige."

"It could be, I admit that much." Paige sighed. "He's barely old enough to have had any involvement back then."

"You said he caught you looking in his truck?"

"Unfortunately, yes. I didn't see him come out of the restroom. He called to me from across the parking lot. But I covered my ..."

"Nosy, illegal searching of the man's truck?"

"I wish you wouldn't put it that way," Paige protested. "It makes it sound so ..."

"So much like you were searching a truck illegally because you're nosy?"

"Something like that," Paige admitted. "But I simply dropped my other arm and told him my cell phone had fallen in. I was taking photos – which is true, by the way – and I backed into his truck – also true – and then lost my balance and dropped the cell phone — not so true. In any case, he bought the story and just told me to be more careful in the future."

"Well, if you're right, what do you think he's looking for?" Jake stood up. "Tell me before I go place the order for your 'non-green' pizza."

"I don't know what he's looking for," Paige said, "but I intend to find out."

"I'm sure you do." Jake sighed and headed for the door, waving as he walked out.

Paige followed him and casually added one last statement, smiling as she leaned in the doorway. "Don't forget: tomato, mushroom and extra cheese."

Paige closed the cabin door, moved to the kitchen table, and fired up her laptop. She inserted Walt Farmer's CD and pulled up the section that detailed *Shane's* filming locations. One by one, she compared the locations described in the CD, the coordinates and phrases on the paper Percy had dropped at the JH Historical Society, and her own observations.

She'd already explored Antelope Flats, locating the movie's old town site and cemetery hill, finding metal objects. And her escapades at Schwabacher Landing had turned up more than twigs and mud; discovering the metal detector in Percy's truck gave her reason to further suspect a connection between him and the metal items turning up. But she hadn't yet explored the third set of coordinates, or the phrase about the cattle herd. Could those provide another clue?

She opened a GPS map program and ran the coordinates on Percy's note. As her laptop screen registered a response to the search, she drew in a sharp breath. The location was just east of Jake's ranch.

CHAPTER EIGHTEEN

The Blue Sky Café filled up quickly that morning. Regulars stopped by for their usual to go orders on the way to jobs around town. Others claimed tables, lingering over breakfast bagel sandwiches and omelets. A few customers spilled over into the outdoor patio, keeping jackets on to fight the early morning chill as they sipped coffee and nibbled on freshly baked muffins and scones.

Paige found herself already recognizing return customers. She glanced around as she stocked the display case with blueberry scones. Early season tourists occupied a few of the indoor tables, their T-shirt logos indicating other travel spots they'd visited – national parks like Grand Canyon and Yosemite, popular areas such as Charleston and New Orleans, or simply hometown sports teams. Outside, a cluster of teenage girls chatted over lattes. A forty-something woman with stylish, short silver-grey hair ordered herbal tea from Sara at the window counter, and then took a seat, setting a paper journal and pen next to her tea.

Finished stocking the display case, Paige took over at the main register, greeting customers, filling breakfast orders, and handing out change. The buzz of activity kept Paige busy, but wasn't enough to keep her thoughts off her online search the night before. If it hadn't been dark and Jake wasn't on his way home with pizza, Paige might have headed straight to the spot of the third coordinates after she found them through her map program. Instead, she had forced the yearning aside.

Pizza and a good night's rest was a wiser choice since she had to be at the café early in the morning.

"A scone for your thoughts," Judy said. She nudged Paige with her elbow as she packed a "to go" order of apple fritters for a law office.

"I'm sorry, Judy," Paige said. "I know I'm quiet today. I just can't get my mind off ..." She paused, considering her words as she restocked a plate with fresh cinnamon rolls. "... that article I'm working on."

"The one on the western movies filmed in Jackson Hole?"

"Exactly, especially the particulars of *Shane*," Paige said.

Judy looked across the counter, surveying the room. "You ought to go talk to Ray Rowland, the man sitting by the window."

Paige followed Judy's gaze. "The older gentleman with the blue jacket and cowboy hat on the other chair? Any particular reason?"

Judy shrugged. "Just that he's been around here his whole life. When was *Shane* filmed? Early fifties?"

"Yes, 1951," Paige said. The conversation paused while Paige served a caramel coffee and apple-bran muffin to a customer in line.

"Well, he was certainly here then," Judy continued. "He must be close to ninety. Maybe eighty-five, I'm not sure. Go on, take a short break." Judy nodded her head toward the man.

"Are you sure?" Paige asked. Although now eager, she didn't want to take advantage.

"Of course," Judy said. "It's been a busy morning, but there are only a few people in line now. Go. Take ten."

Paige took off her apron, set it in the back room, and washed her hands. Trying not to get her hopes up, she reminded herself that plenty of people lived in Jackson in the fifties, and very few would have been involved with the filming. Still, it was worth following any potential lead. She returned to the front of the café and approached the man Judy had indicated.

"Mr. Rowland?"

The man looked up at Paige, his eyebrows furrowed. For a brief moment, Paige was sorry she'd followed Judy's suggestion. She'd disturbed a customer enjoying his coffee. It occurred to her that she should have at least brought over a pot to offer a refill. That would have been a smart, though somewhat sneaky, way to approach the man. Fortunately his eyebrows relaxed, and a smile crossed his face.

"Mr. Rowland is my father, may he rest in peace. My name is Ray." He lifted his jacket and hat off the other chair and motioned for Paige to sit.

Paige breathed a sigh of relief, but still paused before sitting down. "I don't want to interrupt."

"Too late for that, pretty lady," Ray said, his voice gruff, but with an accompanying smile that hinted of teasing.

Paige sat down and rested her forearms against the table, hands clasped. Taking a closer look at the weathered face across from her, she guessed Judy's age approximation was about right. Ray Rowland was well past eighty, perhaps closer to ninety. A carved cane resting by the window helped confirm her calculation. The man was slight, almost frail.

What little hair he sported was combed to one side in wispy silver strands.

"A pleasure to meet you, Mr... Ray," Paige said. "My name is Paige MacKenzie, and Judy suggested I stop by your table to say hello."

"You're a history buff, I take it." Ray took a sip of coffee.

"Well, sort of," Paige said. "What makes you say that?"

Ray harrumphed. "Why else would you want to talk to an old codger like me?" He reached across the table and tapped on Paige's hand in a grandfatherly way. "Go on, ask me anything you want. I've been here since the Civil War, or maybe it's the Revolutionary War, now that I think back."

Paige grinned. "I'm guessing closer to World War Two, maybe not even that far back."

"Aren't you a sweet-talker," Ray said. "No, I was around before that. Our family homesteaded here in the late 1800s. I joined the batch of 'em in the thirties – meaning the *1930s*, mind you, not the 1830s." He chuckled and raised his coffee cup to his lips.

"I don't know ..." Paige said, playing along. "It seems you were just telling me about the Revolutionary War." She was quickly taking a liking to the local character.

"All right, I admit I was exaggerating just a tiny bit before," Ray said.

"Just a tiny bit," Paige repeated, smiling.

"So what is it you want to know?"

"I'm working on an article about movies that were filmed in this area," Paige said.

"Well, you picked a fine subject there. Plenty of movies have been filmed here in Jackson Hole." Ray straightened his back. "*The Big Trail* is one great example, especially if you're a John Wayne fan. *Bad Bascomb* is another one, though I was just a youngster back in the forties, when it was filmed. Wallace Berry was in that one, and Margaret O'Brien. She was always cute as the dickens."

Paige smiled at the quaint expression. Her own grandfather had often referred to her the same way.

"And don't forget *Spencer's Mountain*," Ray added. "You ought to check with Margene Jensen about that one. She dated Henry Fonda while that was filming here, you know. You can find her over at West Lives On Gallery, across the street from the Wort. Or you might catch her at The Silver Dollar. She meets friends there sometimes for lunch, or later in the day."

"Great suggestion, thank you," Paige said. "I remember seeing a picture of them in the hallway of the hotel. Right now I'm especially interested in the movie, *Shane*. Judy suggested you might have some recollections about that period of time."

"Ah, *Shane*." Ray nodded. "Now there's a true western. They don't make 'em like that anymore. I loved that movie, still do."

"It's fabulous," Paige said. "I just saw it the other night for the first time."

Rays eyes opened wide. "Where have you been all of your twenty-whatever years? That's a classic."

Paige smiled at the age reference. She was sure he could tell she was in her thirties.

"That was some crazy time when that was filming," Ray said, shaking his head.

"Really?" Paige sat up straighter, hoping for some inside information. In fact, could it be? "I read that they used some locals for extras. Did you happen to be one of them?"

Ray shook his head, dashing Paige's hopes. "Nah, I wasn't interested, and they had plenty of takers. I didn't even hang out over at the Wort, like a bunch of folks did, tryin' to get a glimpse of the stars. They stayed there, you know. Most of 'em, anyway. Word has it that Jean Arthur used to entertain guests by sliding down the stairway banister."

"Yes, I read that on a plaque on the wall when I went to The Silver Dollar Bar," Paige said. "That must have been something, the cast staying there, and locals hanging out, too."

"Oh, it was something, all right," Ray said. "Jimmy used to tell me crazy stories about all that. Weren't never a dull moment in that bar while they were here. Not that there's ever a dull moment now, what with the bands they bring in, and football games on the screens. Always something going on there."

"Jimmy?"

"My cousin, Jimmy," Ray said. "Now *he* was an extra."

"Really?" Paige leaned forward a bit. "What part did he play?" She searched her memory for different scenes in the film that used groups of people.

"Ha! He didn't have a part, though it would sound like it if you heard him tell it. He just helped wranglers in a couple scenes. Always good with horses, though he had one once some years ago that was full of spirit. Liked to bolt off on its own just for the sake of causing trouble. I remember one time ..." Ray paused, as if thinking over the details of the story before telling it.

"I'd love to talk to him about those filming days," Paige said, bringing the conversation back around, but hoping she wasn't being too rude. She suspected the horse story would be lengthy. "If you don't think he'd mind. He might know something that would add local interest to the article I'm working on."

Ray laughed. "Well, I don't think he'd mind. He always loved bragging about being involved. You'd think he was one of the stars."

"Great," Paige said, barely able to contain her excitement. Talking to someone who'd actually been on the set could be an excellent source of information. "Where could I find him?"

Again, Ray laughed. "Up there on Snow King." He nodded toward the mountain a few blocks away.

"On Snow King?" Paige pictured the mountain known as the "town hill." Most of it consisted of evergreens, hiking trails, and ski runs. But there were a few condos, too.

"Yep," Ray said. "I'd expect it to be a one-way conversation, though. He's been up there for a couple decades. Second row and several gravestones over."

"Oh." Paige's enthusiasm plummeted. If Ray Rowland hadn't seemed like a nice man – not to mention a customer – she might have chided him for leading her on. Instead she just sighed. "You were just teasing me," she said, leaning back in her chair.

"A little," Ray admitted. "But not about Jimmy being an extra. That part is true. You go do some research, you'll see. Jimmy Rowland."

"Any other relatives around here?" Paige asked.

Ray shook his head. "Nah. They all moved away, raised families, settled down other places. Kids do that, leave small towns for the bigger world. Jimmy did, too. Had a bunch of kids. I lost track of them after a while. But he always wanted this to be his final resting place."

Paige tucked the information away mentally and glanced over at the counter. The line had disappeared, but that didn't mean it was right to linger on a break. "Thank you, Ray," Paige said, standing up. "It was nice to meet you. I'd better get back to work."

"My pleasure," Ray said, standing as well. He held onto the edge of the table as he reached for his cane, and then used the cane to keep his balance as he picked up his hat, put it on and walked slowly toward the door.

Paige returned to the back room, grabbed her apron, and rejoined Judy at the front counter.

"Did you learn anything from Ray that will help with your article?" Judy asked. "He can seem a little ornery, but he's really rather sweet. And he's been around long enough to know a few things."

"Maybe," Paige said, not sure of the answer herself. Perhaps the conversation with Ray Rowland would lead to something. Perhaps it wouldn't. But it never hurt to talk to the old-timers. She appreciated Judy pointing him out.

Two hours later, lunch was prepped and the back counters were clean. Paige checked with Judy before clocking out for the day.

"Anything else I can do to help?"

"I think we're fine," Judy said, turning to Sara. "Right?"

"All good," Sara said. "Oh, wait. Is this your phone, Paige? I found it when I bussed the patio." She held up a silver flip phone.

Paige smiled. Only slightly more than a decade older than the young café helper, she remembered that, as a teen, adults in their thirties did seem older. But the old-fashioned phone was still from an earlier era. She shook her head. "It's not mine. A customer must have left it."

"A tourist, maybe?" Judy said. "I hope the person wasn't on the way out of town. I'd hate to be on a plane before realizing I didn't have my phone."

"We should call the last number dialed," Paige said. "At least that might tell us whose phone it is."

"Good idea," Judy said. "Then we could call on their landline."

"People still have landlines?" Sara said.

"I do." Judy smiled.

Paige searched the phone's list of calls, and dialed the last number. Her eyes widened as the call was answered. "Yes," she said, hesitantly as Judy and Sara watched her odd reaction. "No, this isn't Percy Carter. This is The Blue Sky Café in Jackson, Wyoming. I was just calling the last number dialed to find out whose phone it is. A customer left it behind." She paused, listening to the person on the other end of the line. "Ah, I see. Well, he'll probably remember he left it here, or we'll catch him the next time he comes in." Again she paused to listen. "I understand. Thank you." She closed the flip phone.

"Was it another local who might be able to find him?" Judy asked

"No," Paige said. "It was a nursing home in Los Angeles. The receptionist said she thinks he'll come back for the phone, as he calls his father several times a day to check up on him."

"Well, that's nice, isn't it?" Judy said. "Some people rarely even visit elderly parents in homes like that."

"Yes." Paige nodded, her thoughts already linking the comment she'd overheard the first time she'd seen Percy at the café." *No, Pop, I haven't found it yet.*

"I'll keep it here," Judy said, indicating a shelf below the counter. "He'll probably come back for it."

Paige handed the phone to Judy, said goodbye, and clocked out. She pulled her keys out of her purse, and walked to her car, focused on the information she'd gained from Ray, as well as the odd phone call. She couldn't help but think there was something to be learned from the connection between Percy Carter and his father. And, dead or alive, Jimmy Rowland was still a new lead.

CHAPTER NINETEEN

Paige left the café with three destinations on her mind. The first: a quick stop to see if Rob Stevens knew anything about Jimmy Rowland. The second: A trip to the county library. The third: a stop at the Animal Adoption Center to meet Jake, as she'd promised the day before. And, if she could fit it in, she'd add an afternoon jog that would just happen to be in the area of the third set of coordinates on Percy's note. It was the one location she had yet to explore. A short run would clear her head, and help her process her thoughts, as well as give her an excuse to check out the area.

Rob was behind the front counter when she entered the JH Historical Society. She waited while he finished ringing up a sales transaction for the gift shop, handing change to a couple who'd purchased a coffee table book of Jackson Hole landscape photographs.

"This is a pleasant surprise," Rob said after the customers left. "The back reference room is empty, if you're looking to use it."

Paige thanked him, but shook her head. "Too beautiful of a day to stay inside," she said. "I'm planning to spend some time up in the park. Maybe take a short hike, or a run."

"I see." Rob smiled. "Well, you'll stay in good shape jogging at this altitude."

"Tell me about it," Paige laughed. "It's going to take me awhile to get used to it, but it sure makes for a good workout."

"What brings you in today, then?" Rob asked. "More research?"

"More questions," Paige said.

"Ah, one and the same, I suspect." Rob laughed good-naturedly.

"Good guess," Paige admitted. "In particular, I'm wondering if you know a local guy named Ray Rowland. I met him this morning."

Rob tilted his head to the side, thinking. "The name sounds familiar. He's one of Jackson Hole's old-timers, right?"

Paige nodded. "Yes. Judy pointed him out to me at the café, said he's been around forever."

"We've got a few folks like that in this valley," Rob said. "You'll see newcomers everywhere you look, but you can still find descendants of homesteaders mingling with the tourists."

"And he's one of them," Paige said. "I had a chance to talk to him during a break at the café."

"Oh, are you working there now?"

"Yes, just a few mornings a week."

"That's a great place to hang out if you want to get to know the locals *and* the tourists," Rob said.

"Definitely. Anyway, I thought Ray could give me some inside information about the *Shane* filming."

"Was he involved with it?" Rob asked. "I know they used locals as extras. Maybe he was one of them?"

Paige shook her head. "No, I had hoped so, but he didn't have anything to do with the movie. However, his cousin did, a guy named Jimmy Rowland. Ray said he used to brag about being in it. He passed away a long time ago, though. So there's no way I can ask him anything."

Rob stroked his chin. "Any chance he's mentioned in Walt Farmer's book? Some of the cast and crew are listed on that CD, right?"

"I read through the names of the extras," Paige said. "There's nothing about Jimmy Rowland, or any Rowland at all. According to Ray, Jimmy just helped the wranglers on the set."

"Well, that makes sense," Rob said. "Someone had to keep the horses under control, and it wouldn't have been the cast or production crew. Can't imagine what kind of chaos there would have been without local wranglers."

Paige laughed. "Yes, from what I've read, Jack Palance was so nervous about riding a horse that they had to use the same film clip more than once because they couldn't get the shots they needed."

"Seems strange considering the parts he played, doesn't it?" Rob said. "But I guess that's why they call them 'characters.'"

"It's easy to forget the actors aren't one and the same with the characters sometimes," Paige said. "Especially if they tend to stick to certain roles, like cowboy villains."

The discussion ended abruptly as a tour group began flowing through the door, chattering with excitement. Paige estimated at least two dozen map-holding and camera-toting visitors filed into the museum as their guide paid admission for everyone. Paige waved a non-verbal 'good-bye' to Rob, who would clearly be occupied for some time, and left.

Paige drove through town and pulled into the county library's parking lot. The state-of-the-art facility had proven useful when she'd researched the area on her first trip. It stood to reason she might obtain additional information there.

The silence inside the building was quite a contrast to the commotion of the tour group at the museum. She sat in an overstuffed armchair in front of the library's fireplace, leaned back, closed her eyes, and let her mind wander. Frustrating as it was to find bits and pieces of information without anything concrete to link them together, her instincts told her there was something there, something she was overlooking. If she could just figure out what it was, she'd be closer to connecting Percy to the hole digging. Or perhaps she'd find something that proved there *wasn't* a connection. Even that might be enough to satisfy her curiosity. Not knowing was the hard part.

Paige thought over the resources she'd already exhausted. Walt Farmer's CD was an encyclopedia of information about the *Shane* filming, but Walt himself was no longer alive to talk to. She would almost bet there were a few details that hadn't made it into the CD. Ray Rowland's mention of his cousin being an extra had sparked hope, but that was quickly extinguished once she knew Jimmy Rowland had already found his final resting place. She couldn't talk to Walt Farmer, couldn't talk to Jimmy Rowland, and she certainly wasn't about to try to talk to Percy Carter. Every ounce of her better judgment told her *that* wasn't an option. Who was left? Or ... was the question 'what was left?" Paige opened her eyes and sat up, looking at the shelves full of research materials. Maybe there wasn't a person from that time period to talk to, but that didn't mean information didn't exist that was directly tied to that era. Why hadn't she thought of it before? She approached the reference desk.

"Are you looking for something in particular?" The woman behind the counter looked nothing like a stereotypical librarian. She had a strong, slender build, short red hair, and bright blue eyes. She wore workout clothes and no glasses of any sort. Paige might have pegged her as a fitness fanatic, or perhaps even a print model posed as someone heading to a gym.

"I'd like to see past issues of the local paper," Paige said. "From the early fifties, specifically. I'm hoping you have issues from that period of time."

The woman nodded, basic silver stud earrings catching the overhead lights. "Indeed we do. Follow me." She led Paige to a computer terminal against the wall, leaned forward on the desk with one hand, and demonstrated how to pull up the requested material with the other. "I'll leave you to your research. If you have any questions, I'll be here."

Paige thanked her, and turned her full attention to the monitor. The amount of information available was overwhelming. There were local periodicals, statewide and nationwide papers, and even international publications – decades of them all. Focusing in, Paige checked for the local paper and found that the *Jackson Hole Courier* was the area's printed news source from 1909 to 1961. She pulled up only those issues corresponding to the periods of time just before, during and after *Shane*'s filming.

Some of the general information was not new to Paige, since she'd researched the area in the past, but looking at it in relation to the film industry gave her a new perspective.

Jackson Hole had seen swift development in the 1940s, compared to previous decades. The construction of a new airport had allowed commercial flights to first come into Jackson Hole in 1946. After the expansion of Grand Teton National Park in 1950, the area's tourism industry grew rapidly, and the magnificent scenery of Jackson Hole beckoned to Hollywood. It was no wonder the producers of *Shane* chose the location for filming. The area welcomed the entertainment industry, too, according to the articles Paige skimmed through. Excitement buzzed through the town. The paper recounted daily updates on filming progress, off-camera gossip, and the comings and goings of locals involved with the film. Understandably, it was good for business, as well as entertainment.

Satisfied with the overall environment the paper described, Paige narrowed her focus to articles that specifically mentioned filming activity, or related news around town. She found several of interest, printed copies to read later, and left the computer terminal to another waiting library patron.

Gathering her belongings, she headed to the animal shelter, where she found Jake sitting on the front steps. She pulled into a parking space next to his truck, turned off the ignition, and stepped out of the car, taking in the welcoming look of the shelter. The building was fairly new, not far from the town square, with a lush lawn in front. She was certain the grass had been visited by more than one canine.

"So this is the Animal Adoption Center," Paige said as she walked up the front pathway.

"That it is," Jake said. He stood up and kissed Paige. "Let's go meet a few four-legged friends." He opened the front door, and together they walked inside.

The spacious main room was welcoming, with a business counter to the right, and a lobby area with a couch and chairs to the left. Toys filled a basket to one side of the couch. A table with a standing brochure rack held pamphlets on pet care.

"Are you here to see the dogs?" The question came from a hallway beyond the counter, where a shelter volunteer looked out. She held a fistful of leashes.

"We are," Jake said.

"We just brought some new ones in today. Some are in kennels; others are outside in back, playing." She motioned for them to follow, and Paige and Jake entered the hallway. A row of spacious kennels ran along one wall. Each enclosure had a dog bed, blanket, toys, and a water bowl. Not all were occupied, but an enthusiastic round of barking signaled that they were not all empty, either.

Paige walked along, reading information sheets on clipboards that hung outside each kennel. Some offered more information than others, ranging from simply a date of intake to more detailed breed, age, gender, and personality characteristics. She paused by each enclosure, whether occupied or not, reading details on some, and saying a tentative hello to occupants of others. Some of the dogs seemed eager for attention; others appeared nervous or withdrawn.

"This is Louie," the volunteer said, indicating a basset hound. "He's pretty mellow. Just likes to hang out and watch the world go by. We don't know much about his background, but he's very loving."

"How do you know their names?" Paige asked.

"Oh, we often don't," the volunteer explained. "If they're owner surrenders, we do. But we name the strays when we bring them in."

Paige nodded as she admired Louie's long ears. "Yes, that makes sense."

"This guy's quite a character," Jake said. He indicated another kennel and waved Paige over. A shaggy terrier mix lay in a plaid dog bed, asleep on his back, front paws curled in front of him, as if begging in his dreams.

"Come see the dogs in the yard," the volunteer said. She led the way to a back door and out into a fenced yard with a half dozen dogs of miscellaneous sizes and breeds. Jake picked up a tennis ball and tossed it. Several dogs took chase, one retrieving the ball and bringing it to Jake. He played this game multiple times.

Paige took a seat on a bench and watched. This was a side of Jake she hadn't seen before. The sight of him playing and laughing with the dogs was so delightful that at first she didn't notice a slight pressure on one thigh. As the feeling registered, she looked down to see a black and white head resting on her leg. Blue eyes looked up at her with a longing she couldn't define. A sensation of warmth spread through her, and she reached down to pet the dog's soft fur.

"Looks like you found a friend," the volunteer said. "She just arrived this morning, and has been keeping to herself, mostly, though she did arrive with a friend. It's not uncommon for some dogs to be confused and shy at first when they move from one shelter to another."

"This one likes you." Paige looked up at the sound of Jake's voice. He stood next to her, and now reached down and scratched the dog behind one ear. "She's very sweet," he said. His other hand rested on a dog standing next to him, the one who'd been fetching the ball.

The shelter volunteer looked at the two dogs, and up at Paige and Jake. "Any chance you're looking for more than one dog? These two are a bonded pair, both border collies."

"Bonded?" Paige asked.

"Yes, they need to go to the same home." The volunteer knelt down and stroked both dogs softly. "They're very attached to each other," she continued. "They arrived together from the same shelter. It would be stressful for them to be separated. They'll be much better off in the same home." As if to confirm this statement, the dog next to Jake licked the face of the one whose head rested in Paige's lap.

"What are their names? Paige asked.

"We actually haven't named them yet," the volunteer said. "The shelter that transferred them here just assigned intake numbers, just some basic information. The one in your lap is female, about six years old. The other is male, a couple years younger. Borders need a lot of exercise, so that's a consideration."

"There's certainly room for two dogs to run on the ranch." Jake said. He glanced at Paige, watching for her reaction.

Paige looked at both dogs. The one by Jake had moved over to stand by the other one, creating a united front.

"If you'd like, you could foster them, and then make a decision," the volunteer said. "We recommend a trial period, anyway, to make sure an adoption is a good fit."

"Sure, I think we'd like that," Paige said, looking at Jake. "I've never had a dog before, but this one seems very sweet, and the other one certainly enjoys playing and seems to like Jake."

"Wonderful," the volunteer said. "I have some paperwork you'll need to fill out, and I need to give you their vaccination records. The other shelter brought their shots up to date. Follow me. I'll send some food and toys with you, too."

Fifteen minutes later, Jake settled both dogs in his truck, to assure them they were leaving together. Paige patted each dog's head. "I'll see you at the ranch after I run one more errand."

"Sounds good," Jake said. "See you there."

"I wasn't talking to *you*," Paige said, winking at Jake as she opened her car door.

CHAPTER TWENTY

A gust of wind sent a flurry of tumbleweeds across the road as Paige approached the town of Kelly. She slowed down to avoid hitting the rolling brush, and to maneuver a sharp curve to the left, before resuming the normal speed limit. A trio of pronghorn grazed off to her right, and a lone bison stood to her left, a dark silhouette against the majestic Teton backdrop.

Paige turned right at the turn-off for Kelly Warm Springs, the same road she took when going to Jake's ranch. She eyed the activity on his property as she approached, slowing down to take a look. Workmen carried out tasks around the cabins – clearing excess materials and weather-proofing exterior cabin walls. A man Paige assumed was AJ, the worker Chris had hired to restore the fence, walked alongside the property, a log pole balanced on his shoulder. A dumpster rested to the side of the driveway, ready to haul away debris. Jake had arrived back from the animal shelter, and was stepping out of his truck. She was always tempted to stop when near Jake's place, especially this time when he was about to introduce the dogs to the property. But she had limited daylight left, and was determined to check out the third set of coordinates.

Continuing on, Paige followed the road as it curved and climbed, until she spotted a wide shoulder on the left side of the road. It was not an official parking area, and there was no signage, but as she turned the car around and pulled over, she could see a cabin. A narrow pathway ran alongside a buck rail fence, similar to the one AJ was restoring on Jake's property. She parked the car, grabbed her camera, and walked down the path, stopping just outside the fence.

Paige turned in a circle, envisioning cattle stampeding through the property. She closed her eyes and thought back to the movie: men shouting, horses galloping, wranglers keeping both cattle and horses in line. She imagined a young Jimmy Rowland, either riding a horse, or on the sidelines. Opening her eyes, she looked around, wondering where someone working as a wrangler extra might be. If not riding, then where would the person be – to the side, or out in the open? Perhaps, but that could be dangerous. Maybe the extras were positioned in the cabin itself? That made more sense. The film scene was an exterior shot. The crew could easily have been inside the cabin, out of harm's way should the cattle take an unexpected direction.

Looking beyond the fence, Paige took in a view of the property itself. Although there was more than one structure, it was clear which one served as the main cabin. The scene would have been shot from the west, with the mountains behind the cameramen, in order to capture the rush of cattle in front of the cabin. Paige walked out to the general area where she suspected the cameras had been set, to gain an overall perspective. Yes, she could see the scene clearly now: the chaos, the cacophony of sounds.

She could also see that whoever was digging the holes around the *Shane* sites had been busy here, too. She took pictures of the shallow cavities and followed the trail of dirt clods to a few discarded metal objects, mostly tin can lids or unidentifiable junk.

A split in the fence allowed easy access to the cabin. Paige took more photographs, capturing different angles that she could compare with the film, and then walked forward. She approached the fence, and then stepped beyond it, pausing outside the cabin. As she already knew from her research at the JH Historical Society, the structure was dilapidated and weathered. The open doorway leaned slightly to the side, as did two windows, one on each side of the wood-framed entrance.

Torn between the nostalgic charm of the naturally aging structure, and the desire to see it restored before it fell apart, she stepped through the cabin door. Bare dirt had replaced all but a few remaining floorboards, but the roof was still intact. Aside from rays of light let in by the open windows and door, the interior was dark. The single room appeared clear of trash, which Paige found a relief. A deserted cabin seemed a likely place for teens to party.

As her eyes adjusted to the dim light, Paige looked around and saw the normal debris of a structure that was slowly deteriorating. Still, a few unexpected items dotted the ground. Rather than litter tossed aside by visitors, or old relics of years gone by, these were more recent – a kerosene lantern tucked away in one corner, a red bandana a few inches away from that, and … a blanket in another corner. She could only think of one explanation: someone had been staying in the cabin recently – perhaps still was.

An eerie feeling crept over her, the unsettling sensation that someone was watching her. She jerked around to face the doorway, but no one was there. She took a few steps and looked outside, unsure if this was a wise move or not.

Startling a stranger who was temporarily claiming the old site as home could be dangerous. But the surrounding area was deserted, the trail to the cabin empty, and her car the only vehicle parked alongside the road.

Stepping back inside, Paige took note of a few additional items – an unopened can of tuna, a can opener, a flashlight, and a pack of matches. Although of course the property belonged to the park service and not to an individual, she couldn't shake the uncomfortable feeling that she was intruding in someone's personal space. She walked back to her car, and headed to Jake's.

Both dogs were stretched out and relaxed on the ranch house porch when Paige drove up, as if they'd never lived anywhere else. Paige smiled as soon as she saw them. Jake was right; the ranch needed dogs, and she had a feeling these were the exact dogs it needed. Both black and white heads popped up at the sight of Paige's car, and two tails began to wag as she stepped out of the vehicle and walked up.

"They already feel like they're home," Jake said from the doorway.

"So I see." Paige knelt down and petted the one who'd placed its head on her lap at the shelter. The other dog sat up and tapped Paige's arm with a paw, requesting equal attention. Once she acknowledged the dog with a scratch behind one ear, it scampered off into the yard.

"Where's he going?" Paige said, concerned.

"Don't worry, he's just exploring," Jake said. "He's curious about everything, hasn't stopped cruising around since we got here."

"They need names," Paige pointed out. "Unless we're simply going to say 'she' and 'he,' which could get a little boring, don't you think? Not to mention confusing."

"No doubt." Jake put two fingers to his lips, and let out a sharp whistle. The dog that had run off to explore came back immediately, dropping a short, gnarled branch on the porch.

"And he's a collector," Paige noted.

"Yes." Jake laughed. "Look at the pile he's already gathered." He indicated a cluster of odd objects – a partial elk antler, a pine cone, and a chunk of tree bark.

"Interesting that he brings them to the porch," Paige said.

"It's not unusual," Jake said. "He's showing them off."

"Ah, I see," Paige said. "Like prizes."

"Exactly." Jake opened the door, and Paige entered the house, both dogs right behind her. "Coffee?" Jake said, heading for the kitchen.

"Sounds good," Paige said as she grabbed a notepad and pen from Jake's desk, and sat down at the table. "I can't believe the open house is only a couple of days away. What can I help with?" She tapped the pen against the paper. "What still needs to be done?"

"Not much," Jake said, returning from the kitchen with two mugs of coffee. "It's a casual event, as you know – some personal friends, a few local business owners, and some chamber of commerce members. Not a large crowd – just enough to get the word out."

"Any cleaning needed?" Paige glanced around at the interior of the ranch house.

Jake shook his head. "That's all taken care of. A housekeeping service is coming in tomorrow to make sure everything is spotless."

"Glad to hear. You'll want the guests' first impression to be a good one," Paige said. "What about that dumpster in the driveway? It's quite an eyesore."

"You won't get an argument from me on that," Jake said. "It'll be gone. Chris is having the last of the construction waste hauled away later today."

"How about food?"

"Food?" Jake repeated.

"Yes, food," Paige said. "You can't have people over without serving some type of refreshments."

"I've just been planning to put out some chips and dip, along with beer and wine," Jake said. "It's just an afternoon open house, not a meal. They'll have something to munch on while they tour the place and visit with each other." He lifted his coffee mug, took a drink, and set it back down. "Why, what were you thinking?"

"Well, as your *official* personal assistant," Paige said in a teasing tone, "I think we can do better than that. Let me add a few things."

Jake raised his hands in surrender. "Whatever you think; I trust your judgment."

Paige jotted down a couple of notes, and then stopped and looked down at her lap, seeing a familiar furry black and white head, along with the blue eyes that matched Jake's. "She's so sweet, such a lady."

"Yes, she is," Jake said. "And she's very fond of you. It was obvious as soon as she saw you at the shelter."

"Lady," Paige said.

"Yes, she is," Jake repeated, taking another sip of coffee.

"No, I mean we should call her 'Lady,'" Paige said, stroking the dog's head. "It suits her personality."

Jake nodded. "I think that's perfect. 'Lady' it is. And what about 'He?'" Jake nodded toward the front yard.

"Don't you mean 'him,' Jake?" Paige laughed. "'What about *him?*'"

"I think we were going with 'He' and 'She' until they had names, right?"

"True," Paige said. "In that case, what should we call 'He?'"

As if on cue, the other border collie bounded through the front door, dropping a clod of dirt on the floor in front of Jake.

"Gosh," Jake said. "Between your digging theories, that crazy fox's den, and this guy scouting around, I'll be surprised if there's any solid ground left by the time this guest ranch opens."

"'Scout,'" Paige said, her voice enthusiastic.

"'Scout?'" Jake tilted his head, and looked down at the dog, who returned his gaze. "Would you like to be called 'Scout?'" The dog's tail began to wag, and he licked Jake's hand.

"I think that's a 'yes,'" Paige said, smiling. "Lady and Scout – I like the sound of that."

"Great," Jake said. He picked up the clump of dirt on the floor, and patted the dog on the head. "Thank you for this, Scout. But I don't think we'll need to keep this particular find of yours." He stood up and headed for the kitchen, to throw it away.

"Hold on," Paige said. She moved Lady's head gently off her lap, and walked over to Jake. "Let me see that."

"Now you're truly scaring me, Paige" Jake said, handing the crumbling clod over to her.

Paige ignored him while she picked at the dirt with her fingers, letting it fall on the floor.

"Like we were saying before," Jake sighed. "It's a good thing there's a housekeeping crew coming tomorrow."

"Just wait a second," Paige said. "I saw something shiny when you picked this up. Like something metal."

"I believe I've heard you say this recently, Paige – quite a few times, in fact." Jake looked down at the dirt accumulating on the floor. "Let's just throw this away now. It'll be one less thing for the cleaning company to deal with."

"Look," Paige said, extricating a small item and holding it up in the air. "Is this ...a bullet?" Percy's phone comment from the café came back to her. *No, Pop, I haven't found it yet.*

Jake took the item from Paige's hand. "Yes and no. It's a shell casing; it's what's left behind after a bullet is fired." Jake shrugged. "It's nothing special, but some people collect these. I'll hang onto it" He brushed dirt off the casing, and stuck it in his pocket. "Let's go introduce Scout and Lady to the horses." He turned to the dogs. "What do you say?"

"Sure," Paige said, even though she knew he wasn't talking to her. She followed Jake and the dogs over to the horse corral, one question lingering in her mind: *Just how old could that shell casing be?*

CHAPTER TWENTY-ONE

"I'm not sure I understand the connection," Jake said. He pulled two baked potatoes out of the oven, dropped them quickly on the counter, and waved his hands dramatically in the air.

"That's what hot pads are for, tough guy." Paige smiled as she held up two thick quilted squares she had just used to take a casserole out. Had Jake waited another five seconds, she would have removed the potatoes, as well. "How about pouring some ice water while I put the hot food out?"

Paige moved the casserole and potatoes to the ranch house table, adding a salad she'd prepared and stored in the refrigerator earlier. She'd been doing research while she fixed dinner, and she was trying to keep everything she learned that day straight in her mind.

"The connection is simply that the guy worked on the set," Paige said, watching Jake put triple the amount of butter on his baked potato than she would have advised. With his lanky build and heavy ranch work, however, he could afford to slather it on.

"But he's *dead*, Paige," Jake said. "I appreciate you wanting to gather information, but I don't think you'll get far with this source."

"Well, I'd hoped to find his name on the list of local extras in Walt Farmer's CD," Paige said, "but I checked again while the casserole was cooking in case I missed it before, and he wasn't there."

"So this Ray guy is just telling stories. It might not even be true." Jake added salt and pepper to his potato and followed that with a hefty dose of sour cream and chives.

"Salad?" Paige said, sliding the bowl of fresh cut greens and veggies closer.

"Maybe later." Jake lifted a smothered forkful of loaded potato to his mouth.

"You're right, it might not be true. But it also could be. Not all the local extras were credited in the film," Paige pointed out. "There were others who helped out. Ray said his cousin worked with the wranglers. Those guys weren't in the credits. He also said that his cousin bragged about it."

"Meaning what?"

"I'm not sure," Paige admitted. "But maybe there's some trail of the stories he told – someone he might have talked to back then, for example."

Jake nodded, thinking. "What about Rob Stevens at the historical society?"

"Wrong generation," Paige said. "Rob's not old enough. He wouldn't even have been born when *Shane* was filmed. I already asked him if he'd ever heard of Jimmy. He knows of Ray, but not Jimmy."

"Well, then I think you've hit a dead end," Jake said. "Pun intended." He patted himself on the back, one hand reaching over the opposite shoulder, the other serving up a spoonful of casserole.

"Funny," Paige said. "But you never know. One thing can lead to another, which can lead to …"

"Trouble, in your case," Jake said, finishing Paige's sentence.

"…something you wouldn't have discovered otherwise," Paige continued, ignoring Jake's comment. "Speaking of discoveries, I meant to tell you I found more holes today."

Jake shook his head. "Out here? Must be that crazy fox who's been digging that den."

"No, not on your property," Paige said. "But not far from here. You know those cabins up the road?"

"That's a pretty vague description for a valley full of cabins and roads," Jake pointed out.

"I mean *this* road," Paige said. "Not far from here, maybe a half mile."

"Oh, you mean the old cabins on the left side of the road? The deserted ones?"

Paige nodded. "Exactly. There's an easy spot to pull over, and a short pathway leading down to the cabins. It turns out the third set of coordinates on Percy's note led there, which makes sense."

"Why is that?" Jake took another bite of baked potato.

"Because that's one of the locations used in the filming," Paige said. "I went back to Walt Farmer's research, and it turns out the scene with the cattle herd stampeding through a homestead was shot at those cabins."

"So not everything was filmed out on Antelope Flats."

"Or Schwabacher Landing," Paige added. "Which isn't unusual, of course. It's not like a stage play, where all the action has to take place in one setting."

"So there were holes up by those cabins? Maybe it's the same fox," Jake said. "That's not far from here."

"And what about Antelope Flats? And Schwabacher Landing?" Paige raised her eyebrows. "You think your ranch fox is trotting out to those areas, too?"

Jake smiled. "First, he – or she – is not 'my ranch fox,' just for the record. But I do see what you're trying to say. The holes are showing up on *Shane* filming locations, even if they aren't close together. So you think the digging is specifically connected to the movie."

"Yes," Paige said, "I do."

"But this ranch wasn't a filming location, unless you've found some other set of coordinates." Jake said. "And similar holes have turned up here."

"True, and I don't have any other coordinates, but your ranch is *close* to those cabins," Paige said. "I think it's enough. A certain amount of connection can be coincidence, but as new facts add up, the connection seems more solid. I think I've got a fair amount of this figured out. One thing that was sort of disturbing was that it seems like someone might be camping out at one of those cabins."

Jake sighed. "If that's the case, I'm amazed that with your penchant for trouble, you didn't run into him. But go ahead and explain so I can hear your entire train of thought, dangerous as that may be." He winked.

Paige pulled her thoughts together while finishing a last bite of salad, taking her time before answering. "The holes are all in or near Shane filming locations. Metal objects are usually found nearby. Percy has a metal detector in the back of his truck. Your ranch is near one of the filming locations, and he was annoyingly persistent about trying to buy your property. One of his hangouts is The Silver Dollar Bar, where

I saw him examining the *Shane* photos in the hallway. And he's been researching *Shane* at the JH Historical Center, and dropped a note with coordinates to some of the movie's filming sites on it. The bottom line is that he's looking for something that has to do with the movie, most likely something metal. And his persistence tells me he's eager, nervous even, as if he wants to find whatever it is before someone else does."

Jake looked pensive as he stood and moved serving dishes into the kitchen. Paige remained silent, sitting at the table as she contemplated the entire statement she'd just woven together. When Jake returned, she looked at him quizzically. "Something's missing."

"I can tell you what it is," Jake said. "In what you call 'reporter speak,' I believe, you've explained some whos, whats, wheres, and whens, but I'm not hearing any *whys*."

"You're right, that's exactly what's missing," Paige said. "And it's driving me crazy right now. I need to find out *why* Percy is digging."

"And you're certain he's the one digging?"

"No, but it's my best guess," Paige said. "It's not the fox, I assure you."

"OK. So, what's your next move?" Jake asked. "Personally, I'm thinking mine might be to eat one of those sugar cookies on the wire rack in the kitchen."

"I saw those when I came in," Paige said. "Since when did you take up baking?"

"Do I look like the homemaker type to you?" Jake smirked. "Chris made those earlier."

"Chris made them," Paige repeated nonchalantly. She stood, gathered empty plates from the table, and headed for the kitchen.

Jake nodded. "Yeah, she likes to bake sometimes, after the workers get settled into their chores for the day. Doesn't bother me."

"I'm sure it doesn't," Paige said.

"And the workers aren't as distracted when she's not out there," Jake pointed out.

"I'm sure they aren't," Paige said.

"Plus, I'm out on the property by then," Jake said, "so I can answer questions, or send the workers in to her, if anything comes up. And she can do her paperwork in peace, make phone calls to suppliers, that sort of thing. She usually takes the cookies out to the workers during their break. It makes sense."

"Yes, I can see it does," Paige said matter-of-factly. She set the dishes in the kitchen sink, packed up her laptop, and headed for the front door, giving Jake a quick kiss on the way out. "You go right ahead and enjoy those cookies, but I'll pass. I can't stop wondering if there's a connection between Jimmy Rowland, Percy Carter, and all that digging. I think it's time I did some background checks on a few people."

"Dead or alive?" Jake asked.

"Both," Paige called over her shoulder.

CHAPTER TWENTY-TWO

Paige sighed, shook off her curiosity, and focused her attention back on the article for *The Manhattan Post*. Although her personal interest now centered on *Shane*, Susan's last email had encouraged her to weave in other movies filmed in the area. She pulled together tidbits of trivia that might interest readers. *Any Which Way You Can*, Clint Eastwood's 1980 film, featured a fight scene in the town square that included shots of the famous antler arches, followed by a bar scene in the Million Dollar Cowboy Bar with Glen Campbell performing – not a far stretch fictionally for a venue that has actually hosted musical stars such as Willie Nelson, Waylon Jennings, and Tanya Tucker. And Sylvester Stallone didn't actually train in the frozen Siberian tundra in *Rocky IV*. Rather, he got in shape in the wintery landscape of Jackson Hole to prepare for taking on Ivan Drago on Christmas Day. The cabin he lived in no longer existed, but several farmhouses he jogged by in the movie still stood on Mormon Row.

Adding several other references from *The Big Sky*, *Son of Lassie*, and the more recent Quentin Tarantino film, *Django Unchained*, Paige closed out the article and saved it to a folder for revision later. She'd still need to add references to *Spencer's Mountain*, which was bound to be interesting to readers. Perhaps she could track down Margene Jensen, as Ray Rowland had suggested.

Grabbing her keys, a jacket, and a notebook, Paige drove into town. She found a parking space directly in front of West

Lives On Gallery, but found the gallery itself closed. She pulled her cell phone out of her pocket, noted the late afternoon time, and realized she'd missed the posted business hours. Pausing, she looked across the street at the entrance to The Wort Hotel, and remembered Ray Rowland's comment that Margene sometimes met friends at The Silver Dollar. It was worth a try.

Paige's second visit to the historic watering hole impressed her as much as the first. She noted the exquisite tooled leatherwork above the bar countertop, which had been out of her line of sight on her previous visit, when she and Jake were seated on bar stools. Gold frames throughout the expansive room showcased bright paintings of saloon girls and cowboys by artist Ray McCarty. In particular, a painting of card-holding gamblers caught her attention. She could almost imagine them sitting at the original Wort Hotel blackjack table, displayed in the hallway just outside, not far from the movie photos she'd seen before.

Since Paige had only seen a fifty-year-old photo of Margene Jensen with Henry Fonda, she expected she'd have to ask someone to point her out. Yet one glance at the elegant western-style woman at the first table told Paige she'd found the person she was looking for. She wore a classy black jacket, a black sweater, and a museum-quality turquoise squash blossom necklace. A red cowboy hat with custom matching turquoise hat band trim completed the outfit. There was no question this was Margene.

One of the most delicate jobs of being a reporter was walking the fine line between seeking information and imposing on a stranger's personal time and space, so Paige approached her source tentatively. At least Margene was alone, so Paige wouldn't be interrupting a private conversation or outing with friends.

"Sit down, honey," Margene said, patting the seat beside her. "I'm sixth generation Wyoming," she said, and raised her chin. She folded her hands on the table, unique turquoise rings accentuating the rest of her jewelry. Piercing blue eyes told of stories far beyond what Paige would ever hear.

"I'm writing an article about the history of film in this area," Paige said. She felt like she'd repeated this line dozens of times recently, yet explaining her purpose up front was necessary.

"Let me guess," Margene said, a sly smile crossing her face. "You're writing about *Spencer's Mountain*."

"Not specifically," Paige said, unsure if this would relieve or disappoint Margene. "I'm researching Jackson Hole filming in general, and actually focusing more on *Shane*. But I do want to mention other movies – television shows, as well."

"I can't help you much with *Shane*," Margene said. "I was just a youngster back then."

"That's fine," Paige said. "I've been doing a lot of research on that particular movie already." *An understatement, if there ever was one*, she thought to herself. "But I've seen the photograph of you in the hallway, and would love to hear any recollections you have from *Spencer's Mountain*. Or anything else to do with western filming in Jackson Hole. You'd help me get a personal feel for what it was like at that time."

"Ah, yes, that photograph," Margene said. "I do get questions about that, as you can imagine."

Paige laughed. "I'm sure you do. It must have been an exciting time."

Margene nodded. "No doubt about that. The cast and crew were here for a good three months while they filmed. They hung out at the Open Range at the end of the day. I worked there back then; that's where I met them."

"The Open Range ..." Paige tried to pinpoint the name, but it wasn't familiar.

"It was a restaurant a few doors down from The Cowboy. It's not there now. This town has changed a lot over the years." She paused, lost in thought for a moment, and then continued. "Hank was such a nice man. He was a Nebraska boy, you know."

It took Paige a few seconds to realize that "Hank" was Henry Fonda. The informal use of the nickname took her by surprise. "I didn't know that," Paige said. "I imagine he was comfortable here, then."

"Oh, he was," Margene said. "They all were, everyone working on that movie. No one wanted to leave when they finished filming. Jackson Hole has a way of growing on people."

Paige couldn't help but laugh. "Yes, I guess I'm proof of that. I've just moved here from New York. I visited once before, and the area has been calling to me ever since then." *That and a certain handsome cowboy,* she added silently.

"You're not the first, and you won't be the last," Margene said. The reflection of overhead lighting glimmered off turquoise stones as she gestured with her hand.

"Are there any other filming projects you can tell me about?"

Margene nodded. "Sure. *The Monroes*, a television series that filmed a few years later, about five orphans trying to survive on the frontier. It had some fine actors in it – Michael Anderson Jr., Barbara Hershey, James Westmoreland, and Ben Johnson, who was also in *Shane*, by the way. But it only ran for one season. I even had a bit part in one episode."

"Really?" Paige said. "How fun. What kind of part?"

"I played the daughter of a storekeeper," Margene said, thinking back. "I even had a name: Margaret Peabody." She leaned forward to whisper. "Friends from Los Angeles called and told me I was terrible."

Unsure how to respond to this, Paige finally said, "Gosh, that wasn't very nice."

Margene sat back, her eyes twinkling with mischief. "They were kidding!"

Paige relaxed, somehow feeling she should have caught on to that immediately. Deciding to switch tactics, she continued. "I've studied the history of Jackson for some time. Census records show the population was only about 1,400 back in the sixties, quite a difference from now."

"You're right about that," Margene said. "When filming crews were here, they stayed for months, and really became a part of the town – even the stars, because they were here every day, having dinner at the Open Range, drinks at The Cowboy, or here at The Silver Dollar. Those were what we call 'the good old days.'"

"Thank you, Margene. I'm so grateful." Paige stood. "I don't want to take more of your time, but those are wonderful stories. I'm thrilled you were willing to share them."

"You should hear the ones I'm not willing to tell." The mischief had returned to Margene's eyes.

"I can only imagine," Paige laughed. She smiled as she walked away, pausing briefly to admire the movie photographs in the hallway again. The black and white images had taken on new meaning, a melding with the town itself, and the people who lived there at the time. It was just the right perspective to tie everything together. Leaving through the Wort Hotel's front entrance, she headed back to her cabin to finish the article and send it off to Susan.

CHAPTER TWENTY-THREE

"Great dinner, Paige." Jake leaned back in his chair and patted his stomach. A few others had joined them for dinner: Chris, a painter named Ralph, who'd been touching up exterior cabin logs, and AJ, the fence worker. Scout and Lady had curled up on the floor, nearby.

"Reminded me of my grandma's cookin'," AJ said.

"Are you from around here?" Paige asked.

AJ's broad face split with a grin. "Kind of."

"He don't know where he's from," Ralph laughed. "He just goes where the work leads him. So do we all."

"AJ's pretty handy for all kinds of jobs, but fences are his specialty," Chris said and tilted her head to one side while she appraised him.

"We should get out of your hair," Ralph said.

"Need to get back to work," AJ said. Both men rose and reached for their hats from a rack near the door. AJ paused and looked down at Paige, who was still sitting. "Much obliged for the food, ma'am."

Chris also rose. "I should, as they said, get out of your hair, too." She didn't look like she wanted to go, but Paige was grateful that Chris didn't need for her, or Jake, to drop any hints.

A light rain had begun to fall. "Be safe out there," she called as she waved to Chris and the two men.

"That really was delicious," Jake said. "I think you have more of a knack for cooking than you realize."

"Thanks. Spaghetti and meatballs isn't exactly a fancy meal, you know. But I'm glad everyone liked it." She cleared dishes from the ranch house table and carried them into the kitchen.

"You did grate the parmesan cheese," Jake called after her.

"That was hardly labor-intensive." Paige laughed as she returned with two cups of coffee. "While the sauce simmered, I got to read the articles I printed out at the library yesterday."

"Find anything interesting?"

Paige nodded. "Yes, as a matter of fact. I just didn't want to say anything with Chris and the guys here. Check this out." She sat back down and rummaged through a stack of papers, all reprints of newspaper articles, pulling one out. "Look," she said, sliding it across the table.

Jake took the piece of paper and scanned it.

"You see?" Paige pointed to a section she'd highlighted earlier.

"Yes, I guess," Jake said. "It quotes Jimmy Rowland. That's the cousin of the guy at the café, right?"

"Exactly," Paige said. Her expression beamed excitement.

"OK," Jake said. "But you already knew he worked as an extra, so I don't see why this comment is important."

"Don't you understand what he said?" Paige tapped her fingers on the table.

"Of course I do," Jake said. "It's pretty straight forward. The article discusses a call for a couple more extras for wrangler help, and Jimmy says a couple people had quit."

"Suddenly," Paige added. "They quit *suddenly*. At least one did. You see?" She pointed at the section again. "The one guy just 'up and quit, and then left town.' That's a quote from Jimmy."

"That not unusual, Paige." Jake shrugged as he put the paper down. "It would be nice if everyone gave proper notice before they left a job, but it doesn't always happen that way. I've already had a couple guys leave with very little notice. Workers can be transient, especially in this area."

"Well, this guy quit suddenly *and* left town."

"OK. I still don't understand what's odd about that." Jake looked puzzled. "What are you getting at?"

"I think he disappeared," Paige said.

Jake nodded. "Yes, if someone quits and leaves town, that person would disappear, technically. What are you saying?"

"I'm saying I think he *disappeared*."

As if to add drama to her statement, a crash outside sent Paige to her feet. She looked out the front window. A pail rolled across the front porch as a bushy red tail slipped around the corner of the ranch house and vanished. "That crazy fox," she sighed, shaking her head. Before turning back to the table, she paused. "What's with the light out there at the edge of your property? Didn't we just say goodbye to the last of the workers?"

"No, AJ's going to stick around," Jake said. "He's the guy Chris told us doesn't start until late afternoon because he has a day job. He's pushing to get the fence finished before the open house. But let's get back to what you were saying." Jake waved the paper in the air. "Please don't tell me you mean what I think you mean. You know you have an active imagination."

"Yes," Paige said, sitting back down. "I admit that. But I also have accurate hunches sometimes, and I think this is one of those times."

"And what exactly is your hunch?"

"That whatever Percy is looking for has something to do with why the guy working as an extra left work so suddenly." Paige pointed at the article again, as if this were obvious.

"How on earth do you get all that from one line in an article?"

Paige sat back, surprised that Jake sounded annoyed. She gathered her thoughts and kept her own irritation at his reaction under wraps. There was no point in starting an argument, especially over something she was completely unsure about, anyway. Even she had to admit the idea was far-fetched. She took a sip of coffee, and then continued.

"We've already determined ..." Paige paused as Jake raised his eyebrows. "OK, *I've* already determined that Percy is involved with the digging, and that he is looking for a metal object, and that the places where he's digging were *Shane* filming sites."

"All right," Jake said. "I agree that those are not necessarily coincidental. But maybe he's just looking for souvenirs? He might be some kind of *Shane* fanatic, and wants to find anything used in the movie."

"Why?" Paige said, as much to herself as to Jake.

"I don't know why." Jake shrugged. "He might want to sell the stuff on eBay, who knows. Or he's just plain crazy, which would explain his obsession with this property."

"Or maybe he's looking for something used in a crime," Paige said. She sat back and watched Jake, waiting for this idea to sink in. "Something metal."

"Something metal," Jake repeated.

"You know … like a knife or a gun," Paige said. "Something that could make someone *disappear*."

Jake reached over and picked up Paige's coffee cup, sniffing it suspiciously.

"I'm being serious, Jake."

"I know you are." Jake put the coffee cup back down. "And I'm not trying to make fun of your theory. I can see that Percy might be looking for something from *Shane*, and obviously this guy Jimmy Rowland worked on the movie, maybe even worked with the guy who quit suddenly. But there's nothing to connect Percy Carter with Jimmy Rowland."

"I know," Paige admitted, standing up. "Not yet. But if there is, I intend to find out." She picked up both coffee cups and carried them to the kitchen. When she returned, she grabbed the papers and her coat. "I don't have time to finish my coffee. I'm going back to my cabin."

"But …" Jake said.

"I need to work this through while all the pieces are fresh in my head." Paige opened the front door and stepped outside.

"But …" Jake repeated.

"I'll text you later." Paige began to pull the door closed, irritated. She didn't need someone to play devil's advocate right now. She needed to contemplate the possible connections without interference. Even as frustrated as she was, she still smiled at Jake's parting words as she hustled to her car in the increasing rain.

"But, does that mean I don't get to finish my coffee, either?"

* * *

The lights at Paige's cabin were dark, including the one on the front porch. Paige scolded herself as she pulled past Dan's house and back to her own parking space. She always tried to remember to leave the porch light on, just to be able to see the immediate surroundings if she arrived home after sunset. Especially with all the wildlife in the area, walking from her car to the cabin door without being able to see clearly made her nervous. In Manhattan, that hadn't been a problem. She worried more about crime there than she did in Jackson Hole, but not about being able to see when she returned home at night. There were always streetlights outside her apartment building, and hallway lights inside. And she certainly knew she wouldn't be charged by a moose while she walked to her door.

She angled her car so her headlights lit up the front of the cabin. Even through the downpour, she could see it was clear. No moose, elk, or other creatures had claimed her porch for the evening. She breathed a sigh of relief, parked her car, and walked to the front door, pausing as she heard a branch snap somewhere in the distance. Of course there were critters around, munching on foliage, or bedding down for the night. As long as they kept their distance, she wasn't going to worry. She had more pressing matters on her mind.

Paige entered the cabin, flipped the light switch just inside the door, and set her purse on the kitchen table, along with the papers. She poured a glass of water, added a slice of lemon and a few ice cubes, and sat down to read the article again that mentioned Jimmy Rowland. Skimming through the beginning of the piece, she hesitated and looked up, noticing a fruity smell. She lifted her water glass and sniffed. *Lemon?* Setting the glass down, she sniffed again. *No, that's not it.*

Standing, she walked through the cabin slowly, wondering if she'd left a muffin from the café out or anything else that would leave a lingering scent. But there was nothing. Returning to the front room, she took a deep breath and exhaled. She knew that scent, and it wasn't from her lemon water, a muffin, or anything else in her cabin. As an unsettling thought clouded over her, she grabbed her cell phone and punched in Jake's number, relieved when he answered right away.

"Jake, someone was inside my cabin sometime while I was gone, and I think I know who it was."

CHAPTER TWENTY-FOUR

Fifteen minutes after Paige called Jake, headlights appeared in the driveway. She flipped the porch light on, watched through the window until she could be sure it was Jake's truck, and then opened the door to greet him.

"You should keep that porch light on all the time, Paige," Jake said as he hurried up the porch stairs. "I don't like the idea of you coming home in the dark."

"I do keep it on," Paige said. "I must have forgotten this morning." She stepped aside to let Jake in and watched him walk through the cabin, looking around.

"I don't see anything disturbed," he said, returning to the front room. "Nothing's out of place. What makes you think someone was in here?"

Paige looked at him, incredulous. "Don't you smell anything?"

Jake sniffed. "Not really. Are you saying you can *smell* that someone has been in here, even though nothing's out of place?"

"That's exactly what I'm saying." Paige bristled, and then immediately calmed down. Maybe she should be grateful that he didn't recognize the scent. She'd just as soon figure he was oblivious to it.

"It's perfume, Jake, a very faint trace of perfume."

"Maybe you left a bottle open earlier today, and forgot to close it? Like you forgot to turn on the porch light?"

"Do I ever wear perfume?" Paige asked.

Jake hesitated. "This is one of those trick questions, isn't it?"

Paige waited for an answer.

"No," Jake ventured. "I don't think so."

"And who does wear it? Exactly this scent, as a matter of fact?"

"Honestly, I don't know, Paige."

"It's Chris, Jake," Paige said, impatient.

"Chris?" Jake looked at Paige as if she'd lost her mind. "What on earth would Chris be doing in here?"

"My question exactly," Paige countered.

"How would she even know where you lived?" Jake took a seat at the kitchen table and leaned back in the chair.

"Another excellent question," Paige said. "I've never told her. The most personal we've gotten when we've talked was about where *she* lives. Otherwise, we've just exchanged pleasantries when she's asked you work questions."

Paige studied Jake's expression. It was clear he thought she was imagining things now. At least he had the sense to not say so out loud.

"We were with Chris not all that long ago. Maybe you're still smelling her perfume from being near her during dinner."

"It's not the same. Scents don't just linger in my nose like that." Paige tried to rein in her impatience. "She could have just seen my car at some point," Paige admitted. "She does like to drive around the area after work." *Or she could have followed me at some point.*

"Maybe it was Judy," Jake said. "Is it possible she came over to visit Dan, and left you something from the café? Maybe one of those peach pies Dan is always talking about?"

Jake walked to the refrigerator and looked inside. "Bottled water, lettuce, and cheese? We need to get you some groceries. The cookies look good, though."

"What cookies?" Paige looked over Jake's shoulder, her eyes opening wide. "I knew it! Those are the same cookies Chris baked earlier and left for your workmen."

Circling the cabin's interior again, Paige began opening cabinets, looking inside, and then closing them again. She did the same with drawers, first in the kitchen area, and then in the back room. Jake followed her as he heard a clattering of metal. She was sliding the drawer of a side table closed when Jake reached her. He pulled the drawer back open. "What's all this?"

Paige shrugged. "Just some things I've found near those holes. I thought they might mean something."

"I guess this doesn't count as removing things from a national park ..." Jake mused. His comment sounded more like a question than a statement.

"Of course not," Paige said. "I know the regulations. But this is trash. There's no rule about picking up trash, in fact I would imagine it would be encouraged. Would you want a moose calf bedding down on this? Or a child visiting the park to fall on it?" She held up a rusty lid from a tin can, its edge jagged and sharp.

"No, obviously not," Jake said. "I just wonder about you keeping a bunch of old metal objects around, that's all. You could have collected them and thrown them away. Do you think there's a connection between them?"

Paige rattled through the items again with one hand, as if debating Jake's question. She shook her head. "I don't think so now. I hoped there would be, but they're all random items, aside from being found near the holes. I can't see any connection. And whoever is digging is leaving them behind, so it can't be what they're looking for. Besides, nothing's missing, not from the drawer, not from anywhere that I can tell." She closed the drawer, walked back to the kitchen table and sat down.

"Maybe you should come back to the ranch house tonight," Jake said, following Paige back into the front room. "You can ride with me, so you don't have to drive in the rain." What might have otherwise been a flirtatious suggestion sounded more serious than romantic. He remained standing, as if ready to escort her out.

"I'll be fine," Paige said. She leaned back in her chair. "I have an early morning at the café again tomorrow, and I'm tired – really, really tired."

Jake frowned. "I'm not crazy about leaving you alone when you're upset, and I don't like the idea that someone was in here."

Chris was in here, Paige thought to herself. She pressed the heel of one hand to her forehead. She'd suddenly run out of energy, and wasn't about to argue.

"At least lock the door," Jake said.

"In case anyone decides to bring me more cookies?" Paige attempted a smile, grateful for Jake's concern.

"For all kinds of reasons," Jake said, "including my own peace of mind."

"Fine, I'll make sure the door is locked."

"And call me if you need anything." Jake kissed Paige gently, one hand squeezing her shoulder in a reassuring gesture.

"I will, I promise."

Paige walked Jake to the door. She repeated her promise to lock the door at least twice before convincing him to head home. As soon as she closed the door, she turned the deadbolt, fixed a cup of herbal tea, and sat back down at the table. Looking around the room, she noted once again that nothing was missing. The book she'd been reading the last few days rested on a side table in the exact angled position she'd last left it. Chairs, pillows, throw rugs, fireplace tools – all appeared undisturbed. Only as she finished her tea and rose to check the deadbolt one last time, did she notice a small space heater against the front wall.

Of course, Paige said to herself. Dan had offered to bring her an extra heater. She'd even told him to leave it inside. It didn't explain the cookies, though ...

Paige walked into the back room again, trying to pinpoint the scent she'd recognized earlier. At least she *thought* she'd recognized it. Could she have been wrong?

Returning to the kitchen, she opened the refrigerator, pulled out the plate of cookies, and set it on the table. Staring at it as if examining evidence, she questioned her own judgment. They were simply sugar cookies, nothing out of the ordinary. Even the plate was generic, plain white paper with a rippled edge – the type sold in markets everywhere. They could have been made by anyone, or even purchased at a local store or bakery – or The Blue Sky Café, for that matter. Jake had been right all along. Judy must have brought Dan cookies, and he'd left some for Paige when he dropped off the heater.

Feeling suddenly foolish, she placed the cookies back in the refrigerator, and grabbed her jacket. She sent a short text to Jake, saying she'd changed her mind and was on her way over. At least she could apologize to him in person, after the trouble he'd taken to rush over to her place. Pausing just long enough to reach back inside the fridge for a cookie, she made sure the porch light was on, and then left the cabin for the ranch house.

Paige turned her windshield wipers on, and drove cautiously, just as she would any other night. She scanned the shoulders of the road repeatedly, knowing elk or moose could dart across in front of her car unexpectedly. Spotting wildlife beside the roadway could provide the warning needed to avoid an accident.

Jake's house lights were still on, not a surprise since it wasn't that late. She could see them from a distance, long before she neared his driveway. Heavy rain clouds kept moonlight from illuminating the surrounding landscape. And it had only taken her ten minutes or so after Jake left to figure out the confusion, not enough time for him to settle in for the night.

Approaching Jake's driveway, Paige slowed at the site of a truck parked near the far corner of the fence, a good hundred yards before the turnoff to the ranch house. In contrast to the bright house lights, the truck was dark, a mere shadow against the dark background. There was no sign of a headlamp alongside the fence, which would have indicated AJ was still working. Paige tried to remember the exact shape of

Percy's truck. She scolded herself momentarily for thinking all pickup trucks looked alike. And why would Percy park that close to Jake's property after being told to stay away? Perhaps it was AJ's truck, after all. He might have gone into town with other members of the work crew, might have planned to down a few beers at The Cowboy. Whether anticipating two beers or ten, it was smart for him to leave his truck behind.

Paige started to continue on, but braked again at the reflection of something shiny on the ground beside the truck. She pulled over and turned off the ignition but kept her headlights on, hoping to see more clearly. Checking for wildlife, she determined it was safe to step out of the car. She crossed the road, dodging puddles, and approached the truck. Peering in the window, as well as in the truck bed, she saw nothing that identified the vehicle as belonging to anyone in particular.

Rounding the edge of the truck, she leaned over to inspect the object she'd seen from her car. *A metal detector?* A nervous shiver ran through her. Maybe this *was* Percy's truck, after all. Turning back toward her car, she'd almost reached the road when a sudden pressure clamped over her mouth, and she felt herself being dragged backward. Jabbing an elbow in the assailant's ribs, she broke free, but slipped on the ground's muddy surface when a hand grasped the back of her jacket and jerked her back. She felt a sharp pain of something hard against her head, and what little light there was went out.

CHAPTER TWENTY-FIVE

"You won't get away with this," Paige mumbled. She tried to open her eyes, but they felt heavy, as if weighted down. Where was she?

"Sure we will. And don't bother screaming for help," a man's voice said. "You know no one can hear you out here."

We? Out here? Paige struggled to pull her thoughts together. All she remembered was searching along Jake's property line and then ... a sudden attack from behind, an attempt to run, and then slipping.

The pressure on her eyes lessened as rough hands removed a blindfold. Even disoriented as she was, she startled at the hazy sight of AJ in front of her.

"She doesn't have it, Jimmy. I already searched her cabin. There's nothing there but trash." Percy's voice came from a direction to the side.

Jimmy? Paige thought. *The fence guy is Jimmy ... Rowland?* No, that didn't make sense, not that anything was making sense at the moment. He was far too young. Besides, Jimmy Rowland was dead. "Jimmy ... Rowland?" Paige muttered out loud. "No, your name is AJ."

"That's Andrew James to you," the man spat back.

"Andrew James ..." Paige's speech slurred as she repeated the name.

"*Rowland*," Percy quipped. "Andrew James Rowland. As much of a snoop as you are, I would think you'd have already figured that out."

"Curiosity sure outweighs this one's intelligence," the man now identified as Andrew James Rowland said.

An absurd thought crossed Paige's mind as she started to put things together: she was sorry she'd fed this jerk her homemade spaghetti and meatballs.

As her vision became sharper, Paige looked around her, noting familiar surroundings – weathered logs, a dilapidated window frame, loose boards, and bare ground. Out of the corner of her eye, she spotted a kerosene lamp and a red bandana. She was in the cabin used in the cattle herd scene in the film. Panic began to set in as the location registered. They were right; no one would be able to hear her if she called out.

"Did you find it?" Percy said.

"Nope," AJ said. "I already searched the stupid trouble-maker before she woke up." His gaze lowered, his eyes skimming Paige's body. A faint smile crossed the man's face as he looked back up.

Paige shuddered at the thought of the man's hands searching her. As she shook off the disgusting feeling of being violated, along with the awareness that it could have been unspeakably worse, the obvious question crossed her mind: what were they looking for? And why bring her here? They couldn't have found much on her. She hadn't been carrying a purse, and her pockets held only a driver's license with a New York address, a small amount of cash that she always carried for emergencies, a tube of lip balm, and her car keys. She tried to reach for her pockets, but quickly realized her hands were tied.

"I don't have anything you could want," Paige said. "What did you think you'd find that was worth dragging me out here?"

AJ reached in and cupped his hand firmly under Paige's chin, causing her to wince with pain. "Don't play stupid with me, you scrawny thing. You know what we're looking for."

In spite of her fear, Paige bristled at his words. *Scrawny thing?* She jogged regularly to stay slender, but scrawny? That was just insulting. To top it off, Percy laughed.

"Scrawny is right," Percy smirked. "You're lucky there's no meat on your bones, or AJ might have been looking for more than the casing."

Although indignant at Percy's remarks, Paige ignored the insinuation, picking up on the last part of his comment. "What casing?"

A sudden, sharp pain jolted her as a rough hand slapped her face. She shook her head, trying to focus. This time it was Percy's face that registered when she opened her eyes.

"He told you not to play stupid." Percy sneered, and pointed an accusatory finger in Paige's face. "You've been searching everywhere we've been, following the holes, collecting scraps of metal. And do you really think I bought your idiotic cover story at Schwabacher Landing? I knew you were snooping in the back of my truck. You saw that metal detector."

"And you were snooping around my place, digging through my drawers, so maybe we're even. And you didn't find anything!" Paige shouted, finding her voice. "Maybe there was nothing to find."

AJ turned to Percy. "You know what? I bet she's right. I should have figured all along this was just another wild story from your lunatic father!"

"You don't know that," Percy barked. "Even your own grandfather said they shot that stupid horse wrangler."

"Because he believed your dad," AJ insisted. "The way I heard the story, they were too drunk to know what they did or didn't do. Maybe the guy just split, quit and left town, got sick of all those late night bar fights."

"Or maybe one of those bar fights went too far, and the wrangler who supposedly left town is buried around here, who-knows-where," Percy said. "And that shell casing – the one your grandfather was stupid enough to *keep* and then *lose* during some scene they filmed – he didn't even know *which* scene – is going to turn up and ruin both our family names. You may have trouble finding work, my man. And my Pop is going to die disgraced instead of peaceful." He turned to Paige. "If your *sweetheart* hadn't started construction, it might never have shown up. Some things are better off left buried."

"Especially if they never existed to begin with," AJ said, shaking his head. "I can't believe I fell for your warped fantasy. I just got so … Just let her go, Percy. She doesn't have anything to do with this."

"It's a little too late for that now, don't you think?" Percy said. "She knows too much, thanks to your big mouth."

"Don't be an idiot, Percy. There never was a crime to begin with," AJ huffed.

"Maybe not then," a stern voice boomed. All eyes turned to the door, where Sheriff Parker stood, gun drawn. "But bringing someone up here against her will is."

Paige felt herself exhale at the sight of the sheriff, accompanied by Deputy Barnett.

"On the ground, both of you," the sheriff said, waving the gun at the two men. "Now! Face down, arms over your heads. And don't try anything stupid. This gun doesn't shoot movie studio blanks." Percy and AJ clasped their hands behind their heads, and dropped to their knees.

"All the way down," Sheriff Parker said.

Paige felt a strange sense of satisfaction as she watched the two men fall forward, their faces smacking the dirt. The deputy moved quickly, pulling each of Percy's hands down behind his back, and securing them with handcuffs. He did the same with AJ.

"I can help this nice young lady, now that she's safe from you two idiots." Sheriff Parker barked at the two men. He then turned to Paige and removed the knotted rope around her ankles, as well as the ties holding her arms back. She thanked him as he helped her to her feet.

Paige stood, her legs unsteady. She looked down at her wrists, both red and sore from the tight binding, and rubbed them lightly.

"Are you all right?" Sheriff Parker asked. "Did they hurt you?"

Paige shook her head. "No, they didn't hurt me, just scared me half to death."

"What did they want?' The sheriff scratched his head, looking around as if the odd scene would explain the chain of events.

"They think I have something that could incriminate them. Wait," Paige said, her mind still fuzzy. "Not them.

Their father and grandfather. I think. I'm not exactly sure." She reached up with one hand to rub her head, and winced.

"Why would they think you'd have something?" Sheriff Parker frowned.

Paige sighed and closed her eyes, leaned against the log wall. Suddenly too exhausted to remain standing, she started to slide down toward the ground. Sheriff Parker caught her with both hands, steadying her.

"I think I can explain that."

Paige opened her eyes at the sound of Jake's voice. The sight of him standing in the doorway first struck her as an apparition, but as he crossed the cabin quickly and took her in his arms, she knew he was really there.

"She's been researching western filming in the area," Jake said. "These guys were apparently involved with *Shane*. At least Percy was or someone he knows was." He looked over at AJ. "I have no idea how he's involved."

"And do you have what they were looking for?" Sheriff Parker asked, directing his question at Paige. Deputy Barnett pulled a notepad and pen out of his pocket, ready to record any useful information.

"No." "Yes." Paige and Jake spoke at the same time.

"I think this is what you want," Jake said. He reached in his pocket, and pulled out the shell casing. "At least, I think it's what they've been looking for."

Sheriff Parker eyed the casing with curiosity as Jake handed it over. "A bullet casing. I'll have forensics check this out."

"I told you!" Percy sputtered at AJ. "Now Pop is going to get dragged down for this. He's too old to take the stress.

You're lucky your grandfather's already dead. He's the one who dumped that stupid wrangler's body up in the mountains."

"Just shut up, Percy," AJ muttered.

"Both of you idiots in the patrol car," Sheriff Parker ordered. "We'll discuss this down at the station. My fine deputy here will be delighted to escort you."

Deputy Barnett jerked both men to their feet, and directed them outside. Paige could hear Percy and AJ still arguing with each other as the deputy put them in the patrol car and slammed the vehicle's door.

"What about Chris?" Paige asked.

"What do you mean?" Jake was next to Paige, wrapping his arm around her waist to help keep her upright.

"Percy said she showed him where my cabin was. And, oh! He was *in* my cabin." She shuddered.

"You're wrong about Chris, Paige," Jake said.

"But Percy said … how do you *know* I'm wrong?"

"I'll explain later." He kissed her temple and started to move her to the door.

Sheriff Parker turned back to Paige and Jake. "We may need to ask you questions," he said to Paige. "But right now I suggest letting Jake take you home to rest." He tipped his hat and stepped aside while Jake walked Paige out. He then joined the deputy in the patrol car, and drove away.

"You're not going to insist on going to the station to get to the bottom of this, are you?" Jake said as he helped Paige to his truck. "Because I'm not taking you there, even if you want me to."

Paige shook her head. "No, just take me home with you."

And it was true. All she wanted was to be at the ranch house, safe in Jake's arms. At that moment, nothing else mattered.

CHAPTER TWENTY-SIX

Paige brought a flute of champagne to her lips as she looked around the crowded room. The turnout for the open house was better than expected. At least forty people filled the ranch house's main room. Others relaxed in rocking chairs on the front porch, admiring the western landscape. Still others toured open cabins, played with Scout and Lady, or visited with Gunnar, Wildfire, and Scotch at the horse corral.

"It's a great turnout, don't you think?" Jake appeared at Paige's side, a pleased expression on his face. "I didn't expect this many people."

"Indeed, an excellent turnout," Paige said. "It's a good thing someone had the foresight to order fruit and cheese platters from local caterers." She nudged Jake playfully with her elbow. "Even the mayor is here – quite an honor" she added.

"I'm just glad you're here," Jake said. "That's what matters most."

Neither said anything for a minute, thinking about the close call with Percy and AJ.

"How did you know where to find me, anyway?" Paige asked.

"From Chris," Jake said, nodding his head in the direction of the contractor, who was filling pint glasses with beer for the workmen. Paige almost didn't recognize a few of them, now dressed in clean jeans and dress shirts for the occasion.

"Really?" Paige's eyebrows lifted as she turned to Jake. "I was sure she was somehow in on it after I smelled her perfume at my cabin."

"I think Dan'll be able to explain that," Jake said.

"Ok," Paige said, letting that drop for the moment. "But how *did* she help you find me?"

"I worried when you didn't show up after sending me that text, saying you were coming over. And then I saw your car out there on the road, with the headlights on. I figured you had stopped to let wildlife cross the road, and would be pulling into the driveway in a minute or two. But when your car stayed there, I walked out to see why you'd stopped. When I found it empty, I panicked and ran to Chris's cabin."

"So, she'd seen me pull over and get out of my car?"

"No," Jake said. "But AJ had told her he'd stay late to do a final inspection on the fence. She'd just seen his truck out by the fence about ten minutes earlier."

"I still don't understand," Paige said. "How did she know where he'd be?"

"She didn't, at least not exactly," Jake said. "But she knew he was camping somewhere nearby while working on the fence."

"Ah …and I'd told you I thought someone was crashing out at the *Shane* cabin …" Paige said, catching on.

Jake nodded. "Exactly. Chris didn't know where he was camping, but knew it was nearby. And I didn't know who was crashing at the *Shane* cabin, only that someone was. It made sense when we put it together. She called the sheriff. Fortunately, he was already patrolling in the area and was just a couple of minutes away."

Paige took another sip of champagne, and then lowered her glass. "I'm just glad you had the good sense to wait for Sheriff Parker to arrive before entering the cabin. Who knows what those guys would have done."

"I'm afraid you're giving me too much credit," Jake said. "That 'good sense' belongs to Chris, not yours truly." He waved Chris over. She finished topping off beer glasses for two of the workmen, and then joined Paige and Jake.

"Paige just told me she was glad I had the 'good sense' not to enter the cabin before Sheriff Parker did."

Chris smiled and leaned toward Paige. "At first I only told Jake I had an *idea* where you were, and needed to call the sheriff. I called from inside my place, and then ran back outside to tell Jake he was on his way."

"Smart." Paige said, nodding. "I'm following you."

"I waited until the patrol car sped by the driveway before telling Jake where it was headed. I know how a man in love acts. He would have raced straight up there without thinking, putting both of you in danger." She sent Jake a look of light reprimand. Chris then placed her warm hand on Paige's wrist and looked into her eyes. "He really does love you."

"Then the credit definitely goes to you, Chris," Paige said. "Thank you for not letting him panic and do anything foolish." She felt a warmth flow through her at the phrase "a man in love" and Chris' open admission that she could see that love.

"Wait a minute," Jake said. "I don't see how trying to rescue you would be foolish. It sounds rather gallant to me." He stood a little taller, and lifted his chin slightly in the style of a patriotic statue. Both Paige and Chris burst into laughter at his dramatics, and Jake relaxed his exaggerated stance.

"Speaking of rescue, look who's here." Chris nodded toward a patrol car pulling into the driveway. It came to a stop, and Sheriff Parker and Deputy Barnett stepped out. They greeted the locals on the front porch, and then entered the ranch house.

"Sheriff Parker, Deputy Barnett, great to see you." Jake said, shaking their hands. "I can't thank you enough for all your help."

"Just doing our job, you know," Sheriff Parker said, accepting the thanks graciously. He turned to Paige. "How are you feeling?"

"I'm fine," Paige said. "Thank you for asking. Glad the ordeal is over, and we can just enjoy this event. Could I get you some champagne? Or a beer?"

The sheriff shook his head. "Thanks, but we're on duty. Just wanted to stop by and see how the festivities were going. Looks like a good turnout."

"Yes," Jake said, surveying the crowd. "We're pleased."

"You're going to have a great guest ranch here," Sheriff Parker said. "When do you plan to start taking in guests?"

"Probably not until next summer," Jake said. "We still have some cabins to restore, and some more work around the property. I want everything to be right before we open officially."

"People are already asking about reservations, though," Paige said. "We've had several requests just from visitors today."

"I'm not surprised," Sheriff Parker said. "With this location, those Teton views, and all the work you've done to fix the place up, you'll probably have a full house from day one." He paused to shake the hand of a local business owner walking by, and then turned back to Paige and Jake. "Incidentally, we checked out that bullet casing you handed us. And boy, oh boy, did Percy and AJ do a lot of squawking down at the station. Seems Percy's father and AJ's grandfather both worked as local wranglers on *Shane*, and a bar fight got out of hand one night. Another wrangler was shot. They claim someone dumped the body up by Slide Lake somewhere, east of here. And then AJ's grandfather held onto the casing with the intent to dispose of it, but he lost it, and didn't know exactly where. That's why they were searching all those *Shane* settings."

"So that's what actually happened?" Paige asked. "The wrangler didn't just quit and leave without notice?"

"I'm not so sure," Sheriff Parker said. "We talked to Percy's father. He's still alive, living in a nursing home in Los Angeles."

Paige nodded. She remembered that call she made at the café when she and Judy were looking for the owner of the lost cell phone.

"Seems the old guy tends to spin a few tall tales, according to the nurses there," Sheriff Parker continued. "Sometimes they make sense, other times they don't."

"But you have the shell casing we found," Paige pointed out.

Sheriff Parker laughed. "Yes, we do. And it's a nice specimen of a .40 S&W, too." He, Deputy Barnett, and Jake all exchanged glances, smiling.

"What?" Paige asked, confused at their amusement. "What does that mean?"

"It means the shell casing couldn't have been from the era when *Shane* was filmed," Jake said. "It's much too recent."

"Exactly," Sheriff Parker said. "Those bullet cartridges weren't designed until 1990, when they were developed jointly by Smith & Wesson and Winchester. The one you found was probably just left by someone who was out here for target practice."

"And here I thought I'd solved an age-old mystery." Paige sighed.

"Who knows?" Sheriff Parker said. "You might have. I doubt we'll ever know the real story."

A burst of giggles floated in through the window. Paige looked out to see two tween girls who had successfully lassoed a roping dummy. One posed proudly by the steer sawhorse while the other snapped a photo with a cell phone. Beyond them, Dan and Judy sat on bales of hay, in conversation. Paige excused herself and went out to greet them.

"Lovely event," Judy said as Paige approached.

"It's exciting to see the response," Dan added. "Everyone loves the place."

"Yes," Judy continued. "I've heard so many positive comments! Word-of-mouth follow-through is going to be excellent, and that's the best advertising you can get."

Paige smiled, watching the comfortable way Dan and Judy interacted with each other, adding to each other's sentences as if second nature. And Judy was right about the power of word-of-mouth recommendations. It was one reason the Blue Sky Café was so popular. The response to the open house was sure to be a factor in the success of Jake's guest ranch.

"Oh, Judy" Paige said suddenly. "I never thanked you for the sugar cookies you left in my refrigerator. That was so kind of you." Judy appeared confused by the statement, which, in turn, puzzled Paige.

Dan quickly jumped in. "Those were from Chris," he said. "She was about to leave them on your front porch when I walked up to drop off the heater. I told her to bring them inside, since I was leaving the heater inside, anyway."

"Ah, good idea, so the wildlife wouldn't have a cookie fest." Paige nodded, now understanding the lingering citrus scent she'd detected inside the cabin.

"You should take tomorrow morning, off, Paige," Judy said, a motherly tone to her voice. "Rest up from this event, and finish up that article you've been working on. Sara's coming in early, anyway.

"Thanks," Paige said. "I actually finished up the article this morning and sent it off to my editor. But I'll take you up on that offer, anyway, if you really don't mind. A day to relax sounds like a great idea." She reached down as both border collies ran up to accept pats on their heads before darting off just as quickly.

"Of course I don't mind," Judy insisted. "And who are those two cute rascals?"

"Scout and Lady," Paige said as she watched the two dogs scamper away. "They're from the Animal Adoption Center."

"Ah," Dan said. "Your first official guests."

Paige smiled. "More like our first official residents. They love it here."

"As will everyone else," Judy said. She stood up, and Dan followed. "We'll say our goodbyes to Jake, and then head out. You enjoy the rest of the evening, and your day of freedom tomorrow." She and Dan wandered off to find Jake, and Paige continued to circulate, welcoming guests, and getting to know other locals at the same time. Jackson Hole was already starting to feel like home.

In time, she joined up with Jake and walked the last guests out to their car, parked on the road. After waving goodbye, they turned back, and faced the ranch.

"I think it went well," Jake said, sliding an arm around Paige's waist.

"It went wonderfully," Paige said. She wrapped her own arm around Jake, in return.

They stood for several minutes, silent, taking in the view of the ranch, the main house central in the pastoral landscape. Scout and Lady lounged on the right side of the porch, relaxing after the busy activity of greeting guests. The property appeared peaceful, almost magical, in the late afternoon sunlight.

"Look," Paige said suddenly, pointing to the left of the house. A small red head with pointed ears peeked around the corner, a slender body behind it.

Jake laughed. "It looks like we have a ranch mascot, don't you think?"

"I'd say you're right," Paige said. "I think that makes your new archway all the more appropriate, don't you think?"

"Absolutely," Jake said, as they both took a step back to observe the new wooden arch that graced the entrance.

"Crazy Fox Ranch." Paige read the metalwork out loud, the lettering artistically intertwined with twisted logs above. "It's perfect."

"Just like you" Jake pulled Paige closer, and kissed her tenderly.

As they walked back down the driveway, Scout and Lady both jumped up, and ran out to greet them. Scout darted off to the side briefly, reappearing just as they approached the house. He wagged his tail as he dropped a clod of dirt at their feet. Paige and Jake paused, looking down at the new prize Scout had delivered.

"No," Jake said, watching Paige intently.

"No," Paige echoed, to Jake's obvious relief. She followed him up into the ranch house, Scout and Lady right behind her.

Paige only glanced back once before closing the door, just long enough to see the sun slip behind the Tetons, and the white tip of thick tail disappear around the side of the house.

ACKNOWLEDGEMENTS

Though Crazy Fox Ranch and The Blue Sky Cafe are fictional, many other Jackson Hole locations in the book are very real. When in Jackson, be sure to stop into The Silver Dollar Bar at The Wort Hotel, to check out the 2032 silver dollars in the bar's meandering countertop, and The Million Dollar Cowboy Bar, to hop up on a horse saddle for a local brew or a good old-fashioned sarsaparilla. You can find out more about Jackson Hole's history at the JH Historical Society, an easy stroll from the town square. And the Animal Adoption Center may just have a forever friend waiting for you. I found mine there, just like Paige and Jake did. Those who run these fine establishments all deserve a round of applause.

As always, I owe thanks to my amazing editor, Elizabeth Christy, as well as to my cover artist, Keri Knutson, for polishing both the inside and outside of this book. Beta readers Louise Martens, Carol Anderson, Jay Garner, Karen Putnam and Sophia Katakos, all gave valuable input while the nuts and bolts of the story came together. Keen proofreading credit goes to Carol Anderson. Formatting kudos belong to Richard Houston for the eBook, and Tim Renfrow for print. And additional thanks go to Aaron Linsdau, of Sastrugi Press, for providing some much-needed technical expertise.

I am honored that Jackson Hole artist Carrie Wild generously allowed her painting of Sienna, the red fox, to grace the front and back cover of *Crazy Fox Ranch*. Carrie's outstanding artwork is featured at prestigious galleries across the United States. A page following this one tells more about her background. Be sure to visit her website - www.carriewildart.com - which includes a wonderful portfolio of her work.

I'm also grateful to Jackson Hole local Margene Jensen, who provided an inside-scoop by letting "Paige" interview her. If only the stories she told me not to tell could have been included! You'll have to stop by West Lives on Gallery, where you can try to wrangle up those tales yourself.

Like Paige, I wish I could have met Walt Farmer in person. He passed away in 2014, but his extensive research into *Shane*, as well as additional filming throughout Wyoming, provides invaluable information for anyone looking to learn about Wyoming's part in Hollywood's film history. I highly recommend his CD, which can be purchased at the JH Historical Society. To check out more of Walt Farmer's intriguing facts and trivia, visit his website: www.theastrocowboy.com.

Above all, there are no words adequate enough to thank my father, Bruce Garner, as well as Paul Sterrett, for believing in me. Without their love and support, Paige MacKenzie's adventures would not exist.

Carrie Wild Art

Carrie was raised on a small horse farm in Southern Michigan where she learned to respect, appreciate and love animals from a young age. Her childhood was spent riding horses, exploring the forests in search of wildlife, and competing in horse shows. Along with her love of nature, she developed a passion for art early in life. She studied and experimented drawing with different dry mediums including graphite, charcoal, colored pencil and soft pastel. Through her knowledge of horses and wildlife she developed a strong drawing technique focusing on the anatomy and characteristics of each subject.

As a teen Carrie bought her first camera and began making photographs of her subjects as a foundation for her artistic vision. She uses her photography for inspiration as well as an excuse to spend more time in the field with the animals she loves. As witness to the wonders of nature and the countless heart pounding moments, she translates her experiences through the application of dramatic colors and presence in her paintings while maintaining realistic conformation of the animal. Her contemporary style creates a relationship between the painting and its viewer, and encourages a love for wildlife and wildlife art in modern design.

Carrie is based in Jackson, Wyoming. After visiting for a summer, she fell in love with the power of the Greater Yellowstone Ecosystem and decided that there was no better place to be to realize her vision. Inspired by wildlife, horses and wide open spaces, she paints in her home studio at the edge of Grand Teton National Park.

Website: http://carriewildart.com

FEB - - 2019